1976

RED HIGHWAY

RED HIGHWAY

Loren D. Estleman

Carroll & Graf Publishers, Inc.
New York

To my mother and father,
to Yvonne MacManus,
and to the memory of Gaye Tardy.

PREFACE

First novels are the easiest to write and the hardest
to forget. Easiest to write, because the writer with
no track record has nothing to live up to and no
reason to look back. Hardest to forget, because
twenty books and a marriage or two later he will
see copies of that debut (Is *any* cover illustration
uglier than one's first, or any set of blurbs more
moronic?) determinedly working their way up to the
head of the autograph line, dog-eared and bearing
the stamp of some defunct library and loaded with
nifty imagery and enough stream of consciousness
to choke a python. He dare not disown the thing,
because his colleagues have long ears and fiendish
natures and will scour the used-book emporia for
copies with which to torment him every time he shows
his face at the writers' conclave, of which there are

rather more than there are successful writers. And so he is stuck with it.

There are two exceptions, both sad. One is the first novel that is also the best, and which must come to be despised by its creator as a singular freak of imagination. The other is the first novel that is also the last, from which the author must turn his head as does a fat forty-year-old from an album photo of himself in uniform as captain of his high school football squad. These are the works of the so-called one-book authors, the Margaret Mitchells, Emily Bröntes, and Ralph Ellisons who could never be made to understand that lightning need not be captured twice in the same bottle.

The book currently titled *Red Highway* could not be confused with *Gone With the Wind* or *Wuthering Heights* or *Invisible Man*. Based loosely upon the career of Wilbur Underhill, a Depression-era bandit nearly as obscure now as the book itself, it is the story of a fairly unpleasant young tough who charges through a number of banks and penitentiary walls throughout an impoverished Midwest, acquiring an underground legend, until his inevitably violent death. It is the product of a youthful fascination with the snap-brim desperadoes of the thirties gained during a childhood when old gangster movies dominated television. It says nothing new, lacks plot definition, and offers virtually nothing in the way of character, but there are some nice visuals — proving, perhaps, that twelve years of art training were not lost upon its twenty-two-year-old author. If memory serves, the bulk of it was written in longhand during my Elizabethan Poetry Class while I was attending Eastern Michigan University.

Eventually, having been turned down by editors at Dutton, Doubleday, Houghton Mifflin, Viking, and sundry other institutions, the book landed in the lap of someone in Zebra Books' California office, who duly shunted it across the hall to Yvonne Mac-Manus at the now-defunct Major Books. I had submitted it to Zebra on 15 September 1975 — my twenty-third birthday — and it was published in April 1976 by Major. (From that day to this I have never had one published as fast; yet that interval stretches ponderously long in my memory.) Because Major was unknown east of the Rockies, I became the book's chief distrubutor in my native Michigan. It was not reviewed, and until this year it never earned me more than the thousand-dollar advance I received for it originally, but it gave me one of the best of all my editors in Yvonne MacManus and, through her recommendation, my present agent, Ray Puechner. If anyone can be said to have discovered a writer, she did this one; and it is to her that this edition is dedicated, along with her then-assistant, the late Gaye Tardy, who died tragically a few years ago while preparing to take over as editor-in-chief, at Pinnacle Books, which folded soon afterward. It's my way of forgiving them both for retitling my first-born *The Oklahoma Punk*.

Placed in context with my later work, Virgil Ballard is the first of a number of unlikable protagonists for whom human life holds the approximate market value of a bullet. This presumption never fails to galvanize critics, who cling to the hoary old truism that one's protagonist must be sympathetic for the reader to care what happens to him. (These are the same critics who have been sneering at the western's good-versus-evil theme for decades.) My contention is that he need merely be interesting, and if one is to believe the most common remark I hear about these characters — "I hated your hero but I finished the book" — then I am right. On another level I seek to show that there is not a great deal of difference between the lawless and the law-abiding in our society, and that we are all killers who don't receive the same opportunities; a belief that one reviewer called "fatuous and evil." I own up to the evil and envy him the shelter of his vocabulary.

The student of writing may detect the influences of Elmore Leonard upon the dialogue, Edward Anderson upon the style, and W.R. Burnett upon its dark view; influences that are still with me, although mostly unconscious now, and I hope more smoothly digested into my own method. The student of art may detect the painterly detail of the new and old masters whose visual techniques I attempted to imitate on canvas in an earlier incarnation. What a psychoanalyst may detect I'd rather not know. They are always rooting around in writers' ids and stopping as soon as they find what they are looking for.

I wish the book were better. Going through it, correcting the excesses of Major's assembly-line editing, I was tempted to force the lessons learned in twelve years and twenty-two books into that old frame, but I know without trying that whatever the book may gain in technique it would lose in animal energy. Walt Whitman could spend his life revising and republishing his masterpiece. I am not of that temperament, and in any case *Red Highway* is not *Leaves of Grass* any more than I am Walt Whitman, or even Whitman Mayo. It is, however, as good as I was capable of at the time. The fact that I use the same yardstick today proves there is still something I can learn from that twenty-two-year-old tyro.

Whitmore Lake, Michigan
September 15, 1986

Part I

Trifling Circumstances

Shawnee, Oklahoma.

The cold rain drizzles down special agent William Farnum's neck and soaks into the heavy woolen material of his topcoat. He blinks the drops from his eyes, sniffs loudly. A sharp, acrid smell, like burned-out matches. Smokeless powder.

The white frame house looms dark and gloomy in the predawn mist, its slate roof shining with moisture. A hinge squeaks beneath the weight of a bullet-smashed shutter. A shard of glass drops from a shattered window frame, hits the sill, and disintegrates into a dozen pieces. Then silence.

Across the street a youthful deputy sheriff releases his grip on the hair of a prostrate figure, letting the face flop forward into a puddle. He straightens and strides toward Farnum. A loose, swinging gait, jaw working languidly at a wad of stale gum. A pump shotgun dangles at his side.

"Dead?" Farnum's voice is hoarse from shouting.

The man in uniform nods. "Straight through the left eye and out the back of his head. Single-shot, too." He eyes the homely machine gun enviously. In the government man's frail hands, it looks extremely wicked. Which it is. "Them .45s'd stop an elephant."

"Yeah." Farnum turns to look at the house once again. A young woman is seated on the front stoop, face red from weeping. Another one, smaller and more gaunt, stands idly in the doorway, stroking her right arm absentmindedly. She is the widow of the man with his face in the puddle. Around them is clustered a group of men bundled up against the December cold. Some of them are in uniform. These are armed with shotguns and tear-gas rifles. Only the trench-coated figures, the special agents, have been issued submachine guns. All are quiet, awaiting further developments.

The garage door is wrenched outward, and two men in raincoats and shining wet snap-brim hats come out into the open, heading for the spot where Farnum is waiting. Behind them, in the garage, a brand-new 1933 Pontiac sedan sits in the middle of a slowly spreading pool of oil and gas, its big headlights smashed and its windshield shot away. All four of its tires have been shot to ribbons.

"Nobody in there, Chief," reports the first man, resting the butt of his machine gun on the toe of his shoe.

"What about the car?"

The man shakes his head. "Nothing alive, if that's what you mean. The back seat's an arsenal; tommy guns, pistols, Lugers, shotguns — it looks like the weapons storehouse in Oklahoma City. Where do these people get stuff like that, anyway?"

The leader of the special agents disregards the question. He applies a match to an oversize cigar, flips the tiny flaming stick into a puddle. "What about the other one?"

"You mean Ballard?" A high, nasal twang. Okie. The lanky deputy snorts. "Hell, there's no bother about him. He's dead."

"I don't see any body."

"We musta hit him a dozen times. He went down twice."

"Even so." Farnum signals to the rest of his men, who leave the stoop and gather around their leader. The uniformed deputies remain behind, silent and brooding. They resent the way the federal cop has taken over. Farnum gestures broadly. "Fan out. He didn't get far."

The lawmen begin moving, spreading out to cover the broad residential street. The government men are eager, the sheriff's deputies reluctant. But all follow the trail of brown stains on the pavement.

Chapter One

May 5, 1922.

McNeal double-clutched the big truck and slammed it into second. The transmission groaned, the chassis shuddered, and the truck lurched into its newfound freedom. On the flatbed behind him, the squat earthen jugs he was carrying rattled and strained against the stout rope that held them.

The wild scenery of the Osage Hills shot past the window; black, deformed trees competed with the thorny underbrush to blot out the softly curving countryside, closing in on the narrow dirt road and forming a bleak tunnel that stretched endlessly ahead of the speeding truck. It looked remarkably like the barbed-wire fortifications behind which McNeal had crouched during the Great War, and which had been reproduced in the six-column picture adorning the front page of the newspaper on the seat beside him. It was captioned "A Remembrance," and was meant to give strength to the headline that was boldly emblazoned across the top: NINE-POWER PACT SIGNED. Something about the United States and Europe meeting to prevent a confrontation in the future.

Now, four years after the war, it mattered little to McNeal what the nine powers did, as long as they kept him out of it. The newspaper belonged to his boss, Nelson Garver. Garver, a retired Army colonel, spent all his leisure time devouring news concerning war, reading it, interpreting it, and making predictions as to each maneuver's outcome. The amazing thing about it was that all his predictions seemed to come true sooner or later. McNeal couldn't help thinking how much the Army had lost when Nelson Garver decided to go into manufacturing moonshine liquor.

Garver's explanation for this choice of occupation was simple enough: money. He had been investing in moonshine stills since before Prohibition, because he knew it would be coming, and when national law made it impossible to obtain liquor legally, there was going to be a lot of thirsty people willing to pay top dollar to quench that thirst. So another of the Old Man's prophesies had been proven correct.

As for McNeal, however, he himself harbored serious doubts concerning the wisdom of going to all this trouble on such a shaky premise. A nondrinker himself, the truck driver could not believe that people would go on paying Garver's exorbitant prices, Prohibition or no. Sooner or later they would start drifting away, in search of cheaper entertainment, and Garver would be stuck with a worthless estate and hundreds of moonshine stills that would do him no good. But for the present, the driver was being paid well enough to transport a few loads out of these hills to forestall any complaints about the future of his chosen profession.

He removed his greasy cap and replaced it on his broad head. His hair, plastered with sweat, hung limp and damp down the back of his neck. As the air came rushing through the open window at his side, the sweat dried on his skin, to be replaced by an icy chill. Although McNeal felt a summer cold coming on, there was nothing he could do about it, for the glass in the window was broken.

The massive truck had been barreling downhill at a steady pace, hurtling toward the village at the foot of the slope. The white specks of the houses and shops could be seen from time to time as they flashed amid spaces between the branches, then disappeared behind the heavier overgrowth that flanked the dry road. It was there that McNeal was going to unload his cargo, behind the brick building that housed the office of Uncle Bob's Real Estate Company. From there, "Uncle" Bob's rumrunners, in the guise of realty salesmen, would distribute the illicit liquor to various outlets throughout the state of Oklahoma. It was a sweet system, and, as long as local authorities accepted Garver's hush money, a safe one.

It was while McNeal was down-shifting the big truck and slowing down to take the upcoming curve that he found out how unstable the system really was. As the vehicle began its slow crawl around the turn, something flashed into the driver's peripheral vision and landed with a thump on the left running board. He turned his head to see what it was, but stopped when something hard and cold was placed against his temple. "Pull over and stop," hissed a voice in his ear. The driver obeyed, wheeling the truck to the side of the road and cutting the engine. He set the brake with an unsteady hand.

The newcomer leaped to the ground and stepped back. "Get out."

McNeal opened the door and stepped down. A blond youth was standing in the road, a wicked-looking pistol gripped in his right hand. McNeal lifted his hands without being told.

"Step away from the truck."

The big man did as he was ordered, moving toward the center of the road, where he stopped. The fellow with the gun was little more than a boy, though he was tall and lean and determined-looking. His face was smooth and beardless, topped by a mop of strawlike hair. Little lumps of determination bulged on either side of the jaw, which, considered with the straight, pouting mouth, belied the frank innocence in his flat blue eyes. The black revolver remained steady in his slim hand.

McNeal wet his lips before he spoke. "Is this — is this a hijack?"

The boy sneered. "Shut up." He circled past the driver, eyes trained warily on him, heading for the truck. He hesitated a moment, the gun held steady on McNeal, then opened the door on the driver's side and swung himself up into the leather seat. The engine growled, coughed, and turned over, launching into a deep-throated rumble that seemed to echo around the surrounding hilltops.

The tousle-headed boy behind the wheel looked down at McNeal, who was still standing in the road, his hands in the air. The frank blue eyes regarded him thoughtfully. Then he spoke. "How much you figure this stuff is worth?"

McNeal hesitated before answering. "Two bucks a jug. I reckon three hunnert dollars'd cover it."

"Thanks." The boy let out the clutch and the steel behemoth began rolling. McNeal stepped out of the way as it pulled into the road and stood watching as it picked up speed and disappeared around the next turn, dust billowing behind. Then he let down his hands and began walking in the direction of town.

He'd recognized the boy, of course. He'd seen him from time to time hanging around Garver's house, and had assumed him to be one of the youngsters his boss hired to make small deliveries to special customers. He'd even heard his name once. What was it again? Ballard. Virgil or Vincent or something like that. But then, it really didn't matter what he called himself, because Nelson Garver was going to find him sooner or later.

"Three bucks a jug." The tousle-headed young man leaned forward across the counter, hands flat on the drink-spilled top, staring into the bartender's fat face.

The fat bartender looked at him incredulously. Was he dreaming, or was this fresh-faced punk actually trying to roust him in his own bar? He went with the latter speculation. "Hell, kid," he said, smiling derisively, "you're in a world of your own. I ain't never paid more'n two bucks for a gallon of this Osage panther piss." He indicated the red earthen jug at his elbow. "I don't get but four out of it myself. I got to live you know."

"So what are you complaining about? You're making a buck's profit on this load." The kid was smiling too. He knew by the tone of the man's voice that he was in the market for what he was selling. "Three bucks. Take it or leave it."

The man behind the counter studied the jug, brooding. "Can I taste it first?"

"Go ahead. This one's free." As the fat bartender uncorked the jug and hoisted it to his lips, Virgil Ballard took the opportunity to study his surroundings. It was a small bar, lighted dimly by seven of twelve overhead lamps that dotted the ceiling. Considering the quality of the food that must have come from the grease-coated grill behind the bar, thought Virgil, it was perhaps a good thing that poor lighting interfered with the customer's ability to see what he was eating. There were fewer than half a dozen tables in the room, but the ten round, red leather-upholstered stools that lined the bar were expected to take care of the overflow. If the establishment did the same kind of business daily as it was doing now, he reflected, eyeing the single customer passed out across a table near the door, the likelihood that there would ever be such an overflow was practically nil. Beyond the tables, a large, segmented window looked out across the dusty main street of Southwest City, Missouri, and the better quality bar across the street. His eyes widened as the sporty-looking Saxon

Six touring car pulled up in front of that bar and two men got out, heading for the door. The car belonged to Nelson Garver.

"I said, would you settle for two-fifty?"

The young man started and forced his eyes back to the bartender, bewildered. "What?"

"Two-fifty. I asked you if you'd take two-fifty per jug." The cork had been rammed back in the bottle, and the bartender was wiping his mouth with his sleeve.

Virgil was preoccupied. "Two and a half's fine. In cash."

The other man looked flabbergasted. "That's three hunnert an seventy-five bucks! I ain't got that kind of money around!"

"How much have you got?" The kid was becoming agitated.

"Ninety bucks."

"I'll take it." Virgil held out his hand for the money.

The incredulity showed plainly on the bartender's fleshy face. "Ninety? For the lot?"

"Yeah, yeah." Virgil rapped on the counter impatiently. The two men had left the bar across the street and were heading for this one. "Gimme the money."

The bartender punched the cash register and the bottom drawer sprang open. Before he could move, however, the youth reached in, grabbed a fistful of money, and went around the bar in the direction of the back door.

As he swung open the door, the bartender caught sight of the big Mack truck sitting out back. "Hey!" he called. "What about your truck?"

Virgil didn't look back. "Keep it!" He was off and running by the time the two men entered through the front door.

A shiny new Chevrolet was parked in the narrow alley between the bar and the drugstore next door. Virgil tugged open the door and climbed behind the wheel. Miraculously, he found that the key was in the ignition. He hit the starter and nothing happened. He tried again. Nothing. Not even a growl. He scrambled out, banging his ankle painfully on the emergency brake handle, limped to the front of the car and flung open the engine cowling. He saw what the trouble was immediately. One of the wires had worked itself free of the shiny black cap atop the distributor and was lying placidly on the edge of the engine block. Working furiously, Virgil replaced the cable and hammered it home with the edge of his fist. He then slammed down the cowl and hurried back into the driver's seat, this time avoiding the wicked brake handle. The key was turned on and he was hitting the starter when a powerful hand closed on his arm.

Two men were standing beside the car. It was the smaller of the two, a wiry, ferret-faced hood in a wrinkled light blue suit and oversize felt hat, who was holding on to Virgil's arm. The other man, a big brute in work clothes and a greasy black jacket, stood by quietly, a small revolver in his corded left hand.

Ferret Face sneered. "Now, I'll just bet you thought you could get away with it, didn't you?" There was a trace of Brooklyn accent in the man's tone, distinctly un-Oklahoman in flavor. With his free hand, the hood frisked Virgil, found the revolver in the pocket of his flannel work pants, and removed it.

Virgil let his foot slide from the starter, resigned to his fate. "How'd you find me?"

Sneer. "Kid, there just ain't that many Mack trucks around this part of the country. People remember." The sneer gave way to a grim expression. "Get out."

Chapter Two

Garver was waiting for them when the big Saxon finally jolted to a stop in front of the mansion. A young man about Virgil's age stepped up to the car and opened the door. He looked in at the ferret-faced man, then at Virgil, and jerked his head toward the house. "He's inside."

The big brute in the driver's seat got out first, then circled around to help Virgil out of the back seat. He and Ferret Face kept the youth between them all the way up to the door. The other youth led them into the plush, high-ceilinged entrance hall, down a long and expensively decorated corridor, and stopped before a paneled oak door in what Virgil divined was the south wing of the rambling mansion. He rapped softly on the door.

"Bring him in." A strong voice, with a faint hint of Missouri. Colonel Garver.

The door opened and Virgil found himself in the middle of a carpeted study, the walls of which were lined with row upon row of ponderous volumes, most of them, as far as Virgil could tell by the titles, dealing with the history and theory of war. Across the room, a velvet curtain opened onto a windowed foyer. Through this, the sheer pristine beauty of the Osage Hills could be seen rolling and stretching until they disappeared in a blue haze on the horizon. Only the stark coarseness of the dozens of oil derricks that studded the countryside served to mar the poetic nature of the placid scene.

A stack of books stood on a marble-topped desk in the corner of the room, the top one opened to a middle page. It was this page that Garver was studying when they came in. He was a tall, distinguished-looking man, with a crop of iron-gray hair brushed straight back from his high forehead. A small moustache of a military cut reposed beneath his aquiline nose, but it was not enough to disguise the cruel slash of a mouth that betrayed the man's true nature. He had deep-set eyes, and these were hidden in the shadow of his sculptured brow, so that it was impossible to read any expression in them. Virgil looked to his cruel mouth for this.

"'Everything is very simple in war,'" read Garver aloud, "'but the simplest thing is difficult: These difficulties accumulate and produce a friction beyond the imagination of those who have not seen war.'" He closed the book and came around the desk toward Virgil, reciting from memory. "'The influence of innumerable trifling circumstances, which cannot be properly described on paper, depresses us, and we fall short of the mark.'" He stopped reciting, his hidden eyes directed full upon Virgil's youthful face. "You, young Mr. Ballard, are a trifling circumstance."

The two thugs who had brought Virgil from Missouri remained at his sides. The other youth, dark and foreign-looking, was leaning backward against the tier of books on Virgil's left. He seemed uninterested in what was going on.

Garver stood facing the hostage, his hands clasped behind his back. The silver smoking jacket he wore over a black shirt and matching trousers looked suspiciously like a uniform. "Do you know who wrote the words I just quoted for your benefit?"

Virgil shook his head sullenly. The old bastard was playing this one to the limit.

Garver smiled sardonically. "A man by the name of Karl Von Clausewitz, nearly a century ago. He was writing about war. But I think his ideas hold true in this instance. Make him sit."

The order was directed at the two men beside Virgil, who reacted instantly. The brute swung a cane chair from across the room one-handed and thrust it behind Virgil's legs, just as Ferret Face slammed the youth in the chest with both palms, folding him roughly into the seat.

"Clausewitz also tells us that any successful operation demands that we begin with a firm base. Any good architect will tell you that the strength of a base depends upon the strength of each of its components." The colonel looked down at Virgil, who was sitting bolt upright on the edge of the chair. From his new vantage point, the hostage could see Garver's eyes for the first time. They were flat and expressionless. It was the mouth, the grim, hard mouth, that told the tale. "The object of this particular encounter," Garver went on, "is to remove an unstable brick from an otherwise sturdy foundation."

"This is what we found on him, Colonel." The weasely Brooklyn hood handed the wad of bills Virgil had taken from the bar to the bootlegger. He took them and counted them swiftly. "Seventy dollars."

Virgil glanced up at the small man. His ferret face betrayed no emotion, neither guilt nor embarassment. Virgil wondered if the brute had come in for any share of the twenty-dollar cut. Not, he decided, if the weasel had held on to the sum from the beginning.

Garver bent and shoved the crumpled bills into the pocket of Virgil's flannel shirt. "You earned them," he said, straightening. "You keep them." The colonel clasped his hands behind his back once again, spreading his feet apart. "Do you have anything to say in your defense?"

Virgil hesitated. The whole damn thing was being run like a court-martial. He set his jaw and shook his head.

"I see." Colonel Garver regarded the youth for a moment, his eyes like dead celluloid discs. When he spoke again, the Missouri had crept back into his voice. "Break his legs."

The brute bent down over the back of Virgil's chair and pinned his arms behind him. Panic exploded in every part of Virgil's body as the foreign-looking youth left his station against the wall and crossed toward the chair. The ferret slid a hassock in front of the chair, picked up Virgil's right leg, and set it on the cushioned top.

The prisoner fought like a madman, struggling to free himself from the brute's grip. He twisted in the chair, kicked at the ferret, but it was no use. The arms that held him refused to let go. The small thug was sitting on his ankle, pinning it painfully to the stool. The olive-complexioned youth lifted his foot above Virgil's outstretched leg and took aim. Virgil grunted, cursed, and bit his lip, but his captors held him stationary. The foot came down with an ear-splitting crack.

Blue-hot lights popped and flashed before his eyes. Somebody was screaming and it sounded like his voice. His leg, a thing aflame, was lying on the floor, yet he could feel his foot still resting on the hassock. He decided he was going mad. He felt his other leg being set upon the stool. This time he didn't hear the crack. He had lost consciousness.

He came to strangely. The layers of unconsciousness shattered one by one as he broke to the surface, snapping and popping into thousands of tiny pieces, to be swept away as the next layer presented itself. He broke through, began slipping, and broke through again, this time for good. The first thing he thought about was the state of his legs. They felt oldly stiff and straight, stretched out before him. Without opening his eyes, he felt for the tight linen knot of the bandage. He let out his breath in relief. Although the first aid did nothing to suppress the pounding pain he felt in both limbs, it comforted him to know that they had been taken care of.

The floor was in motion beneath him. He ran his fingers over the rippled surface, put it together with the monotonous rumbling in his ears, and deduced that he was in a moving automobile. He opened his eyes a slit. Above him, trees, sky, and reddening clouds were sliding past the tall windows of the Saxon Six. The ribbed cloth top quivered and buckled with each bump. The back window squeaked. He was lying on the floor between the front and back seats. Somebody was sitting in the back seat, his face and upper torso obscured in the gathering darkness. His shoes, the well-buffed toes of which rested an inch in front of Virgil's face were two-toned, and it was by noting this, together with the badly creased blue trouser cuffs that hung over the shoes, that the prisoner knew he was being attended by the wiry, ferret-faced gangster.

One of the shoes nudged him in the chest, roughly. "Snap to, hayseed," came a voice from above him. "I seen your eyes open."

Virgil grunted, raising himself slightly on his elbows. "Where are we?"

"Well, now, I just knew you were going to ask me that question." The unpleasant edge was still present in his voice.

"So?" Virgil squinted into the rays of the setting sun.

"You'll see when we get there," retorted the gangster, sneeringly. "We're gonna find you a place to stay. Ain't that nice?"

Virgil gathered up enough saliva and shot it in the direction of the gangster's voice. It hit his knee and rolled down the leg of his wrinkled trousers. Ferret Face made an exclamation of rage and kicked

Virgil in the face. The sole of his two-toned shoe struck his chin, but Virgil turned his head away just at the right time so that it did little more than scuff his cheek. He lowered himself back to the floor and resolved to remain silent for the rest of his journey.

"Yessir," continued the weasley thug, who evidently believed he had caused Virgil some harm, "you're gonna be real happy with your new accommodations. I guarantee it." He wiped off his trouser leg with a silk handkerchief.

A voice, which Virgil identified as that of the brute, although he had never heard it, drifted over the back seat. "Missouri comin' up."

The crippled prisoner was puzzled. Had he said "Missouri" or "misery?" He shook his head, clearing it of all speculation. He'd find out, one way or another, what was going on. He feigned unconsciousness and allowed the rocking motion of the car to lull him into a state of semi-trance.

A white light burst in his face and remained. Virgil raised his head, blinking and shielding his eyes from the blinding glare. Somebody was waving a flashlight in his face.

"He don't look so good. You reckon he'll make it to trial?" A strange voice, low and gravelly, like coal sliding down a metal chute.

"He'll make it," sneered the ferret. "He's tougher'n he looks."

Virgil was dragged out of the car, two hands supporting his legs while another held him around the waist. He cleared the running board and slammed down on his back on hard concrete, knocking the wind out of his lungs.

It was dark outside. Virgil could just barely make out the tall buildings by their lighted windows, stretching high into the moonless sky. Now and then a horn tooted some distance away, and the swish of tires on pavement was unmistakable. A city, then. A big one, judging by the height of the buildings. But which one?

Somebody got behind him and lifted him to his feet. He was being supported on the shoulders of two men; the brute on his left and a strange man in a blue uniform on his right. They helped him up a set of concrete steps and through the door of a brightly lit building.

It was a big barn of a room, illuminated by six rows of circular lights running vertically along the ceiling from the door to the opposite wall. The old-fashioned wooden benches along the right wall were deserted, which wasn't surprising, since the big clock on the wall above them read 12:30. A heavy wooden counter stretched across the back of the room, with a stout, balding man in uniform standing behind it. A few more uniformed men were scattered about the room, most of them watching the strange procession Virgil and his entourage made as they approached the counter.

Once they had stopped, the man in uniform who had been supporting Virgil on his right, left him to the brute's care then circled the counter.

Virgil could now see the man clearly. He was tall, with a long, rugged face, tanned to a hue like old leather, with crisp blue eyes that stared from beneath the shiny black bill of his cap. Only the lines around his eyes and mouth, and the silver in his temples dared to give some idea of the man's real age. He seemed to be pointedly ignoring Virgil's injury, a fact that was not lost on the newcomer, who knew something of Nelson Garver's influence with the police. The man nodded to the balding sergeant, who flipped open a long flat book on the counter and placed the point of a fountain pen against the creamy page.

"What's your name, son?" growled the older man in his rough voice.

Somebody, probably the ferret, dug Virgil in the back. "Ballard. Virgil Ballard."

The sergeant jotted this down.

"Age?"

"Twenty-one."

"Ever been arrested before?"

"Never."

The old man rubbed the side of his nose with a tanned finger. "Empty your pockets, son."

After a moment's hesitation, Virgil obeyed, reaching into his pants pockets and placing the contents on the counter. Out of his left came his pocket knife, some change, and the key to the Mack truck he had left in Southwest City. He felt for his right pocket — and felt a chill creep through his system. The lump was unmistakable. He stole a sideways glance at the brute who was helping support him, but he seemed to be watching the proceedings disinterestedly. Virgil reached into his right pocket, drew out the ugly black revolver that had been taken away from him by Ferret Face earlier, and placed it on the counter.

The old policeman's face grew stern. He leaned across the counter, slid the gun out of Virgil's reach, and, with the other hand, slipped the seventy dollars from the youth's shirt pocket and laid the bills side by side on the counter's wooden top. He signaled to a pair of policemen standing near a corner, and they came over to support Virgil. The brute stepped aside, relinquishing his burden. Virgil's weight came down on his legs for an instant, and white-hot pain drove straight up his spine. He winced in agony.

"You're in a lot of trouble, son," said the old man, almost paternally. "A bartender in Southwest City has filed a charge that you held him up and took the money from his cash register." He indicated the bills spread out before him. "An armed robbery charge like this will get you sent up, you know that?"

Virgil remembered the bartender, with his 150 jugs of Oklahoma White Lightning, bought at a bargain, not to mention the truck that Virgil had given him. He shook his head, and, despite his pain, smiled ruefully. It was all so beautiful.

The old policeman read this reaction as belligerence on Virgil's part. "You needn't smile, son. Don't think your age is going to make any difference with the authorities here in Joplin. You're under arrest." He signaled once more to the policemen at Virgil's sides, who supported him between them and headed for the door at the back of the station. It was open, and Virgil could see a row of jail cells beyond the opening. He shook his head again, and smiled in spite of himself. The colonel must have been hell on the battlefield.

The powerful locomotive charged down the narrow track at a breakneck pace, its huge pistons chuffing and clanging like a dozen piledrivers. Three cars back, Virgil Ballard shifted his weight on the hot leather seat and turned to stare morosely out the discolored window. He watched the lush vegetation of the bluffs along the Missouri River hurtle past, studied the murky water as it meandered in the direction of Jefferson City. He fingered the rubber pads on the tops of his crutches, considering the possible merits of laying one of them across the skull of the slack-faced detective in the next seat. It would be a simple matter to obtain the key to the handcuff on his right wrist once the cop was out. But his plans were shattered when his eyes fell on the ugly plaster casts that encased his legs. The thought of jumping the train and vaulting across the open fields on crutches sickened him. Things just weren't breaking right.

Missouri State Penitentiary. According to the senile old bastard of a judge who had presided over his case in Joplin, that was to be his home for the next five years. Three, with good behavior. What did he know about prison? Bars. Walls. Guards. Everything else was a mystery to him. Certainly it was going to be a big change from the broad expanses of wilderness he'd been accustomed to wandering all his life. And what of Hazel?

Pretty, black-haired Hazel. He'd known her since they were both toddlers, but how much did he really know about her? It had always been assumed between them that one day they'd be married. How would prison affect those plans? Would she still be waiting for him when he got out? And even if she were, would he still want her? His mind was a jumble of questions, and every one of them had something to do with Hazel.

He turned his head away from the window and studied the dusty floor between his stiffened legs. Five years. On a lousy bum rap. He would just have to make the best of it.

Chapter Three

"Virgil Ballard! Well, I'll be damned!" The short, broad-shouldered con held out a callused hand as Virgil entered the cell. "How are ya, kid?"

Virgil transferred the wooden cane to his left hand and grasped the one extended him. The cell door clanged shut behind him. "Ralph!" he exclaimed happily. "Ralph Moss! I haven't seen you since we ran moonshine together."

"Two years ago," beamed the older man.

"I thought you was too smart to end up here."

Moss shrugged his bull-like shoulders. "Tell that to the cops in Kansas City. Me 'n' Floyd was takin' off from a bank job downtown, when boom!" He clapped his hands. "We run smack into a police roadblock. Whattaya gonna do in a situation like that?"

Virgil laughed heartily. "How *is* your brother?"

"Floyd? Ornery as ever. They let him go a coupla months ago, on accounta no previous record. I got eighteen months to go." He eyed the cane on which Virgil was supporting himself. "What's with the gimp? Catch a bullet?"

Virgil shook his head. "I busted my legs. Doc took the casts off a month ago, but they're still weak. I been in the prison hospital since I got here."

"Both legs?" Moss' piggish eyes narrowed. "That's pretty rare, ain't it? Both of 'em?"

The younger man met his stare. "I fell down two flights of stairs."

They remained silent for a long moment, looking into each other's eyes. Then Moss exploded into laughter and punched Virgil in the shoulder. "That's rich, kid. You oughtta be in vaudeville!"

"That's what everybody says," agreed Virgil, laughing and massaging his arm.

"Two legs! Jeez!" The stout convict wiped the tears of laughter from his eyes. "You must be the original Hard Luck Harry! Imagine! Two bustid legs 'n' prison besides! How long you got?"

"Three years, if I behave myself."

"Hell, that's nothin'! When the screws talk, just smile and nod. Take whatever they got to give. It's a waltz."

"Some waltz. They tell me the guards beat a guy to death in the shower room just last month."

Ralph Moss laughed, but it was an embarrassed laugh. "Yeah. Well, that was his own fault. A screw told him to go back in and take another bath, he was filthy, but he told him to go to hell. He just didn't play by the rules, that's all."

"For that, they killed him?" Virgil was more afraid than angry.

"I guess they got carried away. But that's just what I told you about. You leave them alone, they leave you alone. Be amiable. Follow the rules. You'll be out like that." He snapped his callused fingers.

Virgil sat down on the edge of the bottom bunk of the ugly double-decked bed. His gray prison uniform hung on him like a sack. "Two years, or one, or six months, what's it matter? It's just too damned long! I only been here a little while, and it's driving me crazy. Now I find out that they'll kill you if you act like a man. I want out, Ralph. I want out now."

Moss laid a rough hand on the youth's shoulder. "You'll make it, kid." He sat down beside him. "You think this is my first time? Listen, I been in and out of these joints all my life, ever since I was old enough to lift a gun. It passes, believe me. You just got to wait it out."

"That's not it," insisted Virgil, shaking his head. "As soon as I get out on the street, I'm gonna get picked up again. I just know it. And then I'll land right back here, or someplace like it, and that'll be it."

"What makes you say that?"

"Figure the odds." Virgil began counting on his fingers. "I'm a crook. I don't know how to do anything else, it's all I been doing since I was a kid. I'm also a con. When I get out, I'll be an ex-con. No difference. The state has my prints and picture. I been netted, labeled, and pinned to a board, just like a butterfly. There just isn't any job I can pull that's safe."

There was a twinkle in the older man's eye. "It don't have to be that way, you know."

Something in Moss' voice made Virgil turn his head to look at him. "What do you mean by that?"

"I mean this," said the other, spreading his hands as if to pick something up. "There's this little bank, see, in Dawes. I been thinkin' about it ever since I met this guy who come from there. It's a small town. The only law around is one old constable, and he's nothin'. It won't take but five minutes to pull up in front, hit it, and tear out again. Lead pipe."

"So? What's that got to do with me?"

"That's where you come in. We need a good, reliable wheel man. I seen you handle them big trucks back in Oklahoma. If you can still roll like that, you're the man we want."

Virgil shook his head. "It's no good. I'm gonna be in here for the next three years."

"So what?" Moss was annoyed. "I got two and a half to serve myself. Nobody's gonna move on accounta this plan is all mine. I ain't told nobody about it, 'cept you."

"You'll still be out six months ahead of me."

"So we'll wait."

"We?" Virgil raised his eyebrows.

"Sure, we. Me an' Floyd an' Roy."

"Roy?"

Moss looked surprised. "Roy. Roy Farrell." He said it as if it were supposed to mean something.

Virgil shook his head, uncomprehending.

"Roy Farrell," began Moss pompously, "is only the biggest bank robber in Oklahoma. My brother's with him now, and Roy sends word that he needs all the good men I can get. You're the first. Whattaya say, kid? You in?"

Virgil thought it over. Bank robbery. That was one he'd never considered. Well, why not? It was a step up. "Okay," he said, cheerfully resigning himself to his cellmate's hands. "Deal me in."

"Great!" Moss took aim to punch him in the shoulder, but Virgil dodged it. The older man gave it up and squatted on the floor, signaling for Virgil to join him. He began tracing the plan of Dawes bank on the concrete floor. "This is the front door," he said, drawing a thick thumbnail across the thin layer of dust, "and this is the vault, about fifteen feet in. Now, there are never more'n five or six people in there at one time. . . ."

Virgil watched intently as the plan began to take shape. There, on the floor of his cell, the young Oklahoman studied the diagram that was to remain in his head for the next three years.

Chapter Four

Virgil was standing outside the prison gates when the spotless Auburn came careening around the corner and slowed to a stop beside the curb at his feet. It was five years old, the 1920 639K model, long and high and luxurious and yellow with black fenders and top. Somebody had been at the wooden spoke wheels with furniture polish and a cloth, for they gleamed almost as brightly as did the chrome headlights. Virgil caught sight of the fresh-faced brunette beaming behind the wheel and smiled. It was Hazel.

She reached across the seat and hit the door-handle, unlocking it. Her arms were around his neck before he could open his mouth, and she was planting kisses all over his face. He detached himself from her advances reluctantly, giving her a kiss as a consolation prize. "That stuff can wait," he said brightly. "First, I got to get used to the open air." He threw himself back in the plush seat and inhaled mightily, filling his lungs with the pure Missouri air, then let it out with a sigh. "You got no idea how sweet it smells out here."

Hazel grinned broadly, showing off her milky-white teeth. "Maybe it's me you're smelling."

Virgil reached out and tickled her chin. "Well now, that could just be possible." He withdrew his hand and looked about him, at the clean luxury of the sedan's interior. "Where'd you get the machine? Steal it?"

"It belongs to my boss. He lent it to me when I told him I had to pick up my boyfriend at the train station in Oklahoma City."

Virgil glanced at the high gray walls of the prison in which he had spent three years of his life. There was a movement in the east tower, and he knew it was the changing of the guard. "Well," he said, "it isn't exactly a train station, and this isn't exactly Oklahoma City, but the rest of it is true enough." He smiled again at his childhood sweetheart.

Hazel smiled back, but it was a tight-lipped thoughtful smile. Virgil knew what she was thinking. He was leaner now than she would have remembered him, and his hair was combed more neatly, but he was still the same sad-eyed Oklahoma youth she had known three years before. The only appreciable difference was that, in place of the blue work clothes he used to live in, he was now wearing a suit and tie, courtesy of the state of Missouri. Though it fit him poorly, it didn't look too bad on him. He decided he would make a good banker.

Hazel placed her hands on the wooden steering wheel. Her smile was more natural now. "Where to?"

Virgil shrugged. "Where you living?"

"Picher."

Virgil thought about his home town. It couldn't have changed much in three years. And it was still close to the state line. "Let's go there."

Dawn was creeping into the bedroom of Hazel's apartment above the Picher Print Shop when Virgil sat up in bed and lit a cigarette. Hazel, sleeping peacefully after their night of lovemaking, was lying on her side with her back to him, her smooth naked shoulder rising slightly beneath the blanket with each even breath. Virgil contemplated the contrast made by her black hair as it lay fanned across the clean white pillow beneath her head, and wished he were an artist. That scene needed depicting.

He discarded the feeling as too poetic and settled back on his propped-up pillow, dragging thoughtfully on his cigarette. Just beyond the open window behind and to the right of the bed, a sparrow was hopping from twig to twig among the branches of a nearby maple tree, stopping only to call raucously to a fellow squawker down the street. Virgil heard a car pull up in front of the drugstore across the way, heard its brake squeak, and heard another start up and pull away farther down the main thoroughfare. That, he decided, would constitute the rush-hour traffic in a town the size of Picher, Oklahoma.

The jacket of his prison suit hung from the post at the foot of the bed, its strained seams sending tiny wrinkles outward like the strands of a spider web. Virgil was reminded of another suit he had seen like it, and remembered the narrow ferret face of the man who had been wearing it. He winced at the memory, and felt instinctively for his legs. The doctors back in Joplin had done their work well; the bones had set correctly, and his limbs showed no signs of ever having been broken. It was only during damp weather that Virgil felt the pain. Back in Jefferson City, the prison air had been nothing but damp, and he had spent every day in agony, vowing to take revenge on Nelson Garver and the men who had done this to him. But Colonel Garver was gone. Virgil had learned through the grapevine that he and his entire operation had packed up and left for Chicago just as Prohibition reached its peak, headed for the more lucrative territory of the urban Midwest. For Virgil Ballard, revenge wasn't worth going all that way. There was no percentage in it.

He took one last drag on his cigarette and put it out in the flower-patterned china saucer Hazel had left on the night table. Carefully, lest he disturb Hazel, who had turned over on her back and was smiling in her sleep, he slid out from between the sheets, and, naked, padded out into the living room in search of a drink.

He went to the pantry and brought down a bottle of bourbon from an overhead shelf. He selected the glass he had used earlier, a whiskey-stained water tumbler sitting in a puddle on the kitchen table, and filled it halfway. He had replaced the bottle and was just taking his first sip from the glass when Hazel came up from behind him and gave him a smart slap across his bare buttocks. "Lush!" she giggled, as he whirled to face her.

She had donned a semi-transparent negligee which, tied as it was at the neck and nowhere else, did nothing to conceal her femininity. She looked like Clara Bow, as Virgil remembered seeing her in a similar mode of dress in a magazine he had read in prison, only a helluva lot sexier. Virgil reached out with one bare foot and swept Hazel's legs from beneath her. She went down hard on her bottom, her peignoir floating down into a ruffled position that left her, to all intents and purposes, quite naked. "Sex maniac!" Virgil observed wryly, and raised his glass to his lips.

Hazel looked put out for a moment, then realized the humor in her position, and began laughing, her shoulders shaking so violently that the negligee rippled like disturbed water. She gathered it about her, and, rubbing the injured spot, got to her feet. "You, Mr. Ballard," she said, "are not a gentleman."

"Surprise, surprise." Virgil put down his empty glass and strode toward the bedroom. Hazel followed on his heels.

"Going somewhere?" she asked as Virgil found his shorts and stepped into them.

He slid on his trousers, letting the suspenders flap about his knees while he donned his BVD undershirt and tucked it in. "Job hunting," he answered. "That's something they don't do for you when you leave prison."

Hazel leaned languidly in the bedroom doorway. "There's not much around here right now."

"I figured that," said Virgil, buttoning his collar and tying his necktie. "That's why I'm leaving for Miami."

"That far?" Miami, Oklahoma, was over thirty miles away. She left the doorway and stood facing him. "How do you plan to get there?"

He brought his thumb around in a wide arc in a hitchhiking gesture, then reached for his jacket.

"Coming back?"

Virgil paused at the door and took her chin in his hand. "In style, honey," he said. "In style." Then he left.

"This here's Roy Farrell," said Moss, his hand on the dark man's shoulder. "Roy, I want you to meet Virgil Ballard. Virgil's a good old boy."

The slight man grasped Virgil's hand coolly, then let go. He had jet-black hair and intense dark eyes, with which he seemed to be assessing the blond youth. The Oklahoma sun had burned his skin to a deep reddish-brown, adding to the Indian effect made by his high cheekbones and the color of his wavy hair. The effect was diminished, but not spoiled, by the pencil-thin mustache he sported just above his lip. Virgil tagged him as Creek, or possibly Cherokee.

Floyd Moss, Ralph's younger brother, pushed forward to pump Virgil's hand. He was a big, gawky plowboy, all arms and legs and wind-blown straw-colored hair. "Hell, boy," he said, "when I heard you was up in Jeff City, I thought I'd seen the last of you! Well, if this don't beat all!"

"You look good, Floyd," said Virgil, disengaging himself from the big man's baseball glove-sized hand. All the Mosses were as strong as oxen.

"Ralph has told me some good things about you," observed Farrell mildly. In contrast to the Moss brothers, his manner was reserved. "Of course, Ralph has been known to stretch the truth at times." He smiled then, but his eyes were grim.

Ralph shook his oxlike head. "Not this time, boy. Virgil can make a Mack truck stand up and dance the Charleston. As wheel men go, he's the king."

Farrell didn't say anything to that. He turned and headed for the next room. "In here."

Virgil followed him, flanked by Floyd and Ralph. "How d'you like this place we got here, Virgil?" asked Floyd. "Humdinger, ain't it?"

"Yeah." Virgil looked around at the sitting room in which he found himself, at the expensive carpet and the big new leaf-patterned easy chairs.

"Not bad. I didn't know you guys were doing this well."

Ralph snorted. "Don't take nothin' at all. You lay down a couple hunnert a week, and you got yourself the Taj Mahal. There's houses like this all over Miami."

"I'm more comfortable in these surroundings," explained Farrell, who had unbuttoned his pinstriped jacket and taken a seat in one of the chairs, motioning for the others to do the same. "The time for planning heists in low dives and condemned buildings is past. These days, it's top drawer all the way or nothing."

"That seems true enough," said Virgil, sitting down in the chair opposite Farrell. "I been reading about you in the papers lately. You got off pretty clean in Oklahoma City, and again in Tulsa."

Farrell cast off the compliment with a gesture of indifference. "Those were small jobs, not worth the effort. The pay's low, and the risks are high. Let me give you some advice." He leaned forward in his chair. "Stay away from the big cities. Shawnee, McAlester, Muskogee, they're no good. You never know when they're gonna be digging up the streets or when some jerk in a J.C. Penney truck is gonna jackknife right in front of you. Hit the small towns, the one-street burgs. Those banks are chock full of cash from rich farmers and grain industries. Just drive in and drive right out again with thirty grand in your back seat. It's as simple as that."

Virgil studied the gang leader's smooth features. "I see you been talking to Ralph."

Farrell smiled again, genuinely this time, white teeth flashing in his dark face. "You mean Dawes. Yes, I've been talking to Ralph about it. The only reason we haven't hit it before now is that he talked me into waiting for you." The smile faded. "I hope it was worth it."

"Take my word for it, Roy," piped up Ralph, who was seated beside his brother on the sofa. "This kid's hell on wheels."

"So you told me. But it's been four years since either of you has handled anything heavy. Can he still do it?"

Virgil let a smile play around the corners of his mouth. "You supply the wheels, Mr. Farrell," he said, "and I'll supply the driving."

"Well, we'll see about that soon enough." The gang leader got to his feet and looked down at Virgil "You got any plans for the next week or so?"

"Nope."

"Good. Because you're gonna be staying with us." Farrell drew a slim black billfold from inside his jacket and began counting out bills. "First, get what you need; toothbrush, razor, clothes. Then come back here." He laid the bills in Virgil's outstretched hand, just as he got up from his own chair.

Farrell paused before replacing the wallet. "You got a piece?"

Virgil fingered the money in his hand. "A piece?"

"A gun. You got a gun?"

Virgil shook his head.

"Here." Farrell gave him the rest of the money. "Get yourself a good one. I don't want any of my boys to pull a job unarmed."

"Thanks a lot, Mr. Farrell," said the initiate, shoving the money into the pocket of his cheap jacket. "You won't be disappointed for giving me this opportunity."

"Roy," said the other paternally. "Call me Roy."

The city of Miami was only about three time the size of Picher, but it was much more prosperous. The traffic here was considerably heavier, the buildings taller and more concentrated, and the impersonal atmosphere that had long ago come to places like Oklahoma City and Tulsa was just beginning to make its presence known in Miami. It was an up-and-coming town, and it showed itself as such by the number of improvements and additions that had been made while Virgil Ballard had been marking time in Jefferson City.

But Virgil wasn't paying much attention to these as he stepped into the town's main street and looked around. At the end of the street, nestled between the bank and a grocery store, he spotted the establishment for which he had been searching. He trotted down the sidewalk, threading his way through the

passersby, and stopped before the building marked
STACKENAUER'S SPORTING GOODS. An
impressive array of lanterns, sleeping bags, rifles and
fishing rods was arranged in the window, behind
which stood a young man in a natty blazer, smiling
out at his potential customer. Virgil pushed the door
open and went in.

Once inside, he made his way through the maze
of axes, tennis rackets, and other outdoor accou-
terments, and stopped at the glass counter. The
young man in the blazer had beaten him there, and
he came to a kind of attention behind the counter,
the eager smile still on his face. "May I help you
sir?" he asked.

"I'm looking for a pistol," said Virgil unsmiling.

"Well, sir, you came to the right place." The counterman stepped back and spread his hands on the
counter to indicate the guns that were laid out
beneath its glass top. "Your choice, sir. We have
all kinds, old and new."

Virgil looked the guns over. There was, indeed
an admirable variety on display. Colts and Reming-
tons and Walthers and Mausers and a few Virgil
had never heard of lay side by side in the case, their
curved grips and blue barrels shining proudly against
the counter's plush red interior. After a moment of
decision-making, he settled on a battered 9 mm. Luger, German Army model 1908, lying neglected
between the gleaming six-shot Smith & Wesson and
a vicious-looking Remington automatic. He pointed
out the older gun. "Can I see that Luger?"

"The Luger?" The counterman looked crestfallen.
"Yes, sir," he said, and slid open the glass panel
in back, reaching for the gun in question.

When Virgil had it in his hands, he turned it over and over, enjoying the feel of the hefty firearm. Long and sleek and heavy with most of its weight in the oversize grip, the Luger was neither beautiful, like the Smith and Wesson, nor deadly-looking, like the Remington, but held a curious kind of dignity in its obvious serviceability. It looked exactly like what it was: an obedient machine that could be relied upon to do the job for which it was designed.

"I'll take it," said Virgil. "How much?"

The man in the blazer looked dismayed. "Are you certain this is the gun you want, sir? It's over fifteen years old, after all. Now, this Colt —" he reached toward the sliding panel.

Virgil interrupted him. "The Luger. How much?" He reached into his pocket.

The counterman shrugged, defeated. "Fifteen dollars."

Virgil spread three crisp five dollar bills on the counter. "Oh — and I'll need two boxes of ammunition."

"Yes, sir. That'll be another two dollars." The counterman snatched down two dusty boxes of 9 mm. cartridges from the shelf behind him and placed them before the customer, who had laid another pair of bills on top of the others. Then he swept up the money, put it in the cash register at his elbow, and handed Virgil his receipt.

"Do you have a paper bag?" inquired the other. "I don't want to stretch out my pocket."

Virgil waited for the man in the blazer to make some smart comment about the quality of his customer's jacket, but he remained silent and handed him a paper bag from the shelf.

Virgil slipped the pistol into the bag and placed the square boxes on top. "Thanks." He turned and headed for the door. "Nice day."

"If you say so, sir," replied the man behind the counter, staring morosely at the thirty-dollar price tag on the Colt revolver in the case.

Chapter Five

Red dust billowed from the La Salle's rear tires as it left the curves and roared into the straightaway. Virgil, one hand on the wheel, watched the reflections of trees flow across the deep purple finish on the long hood, listened to the gutteral booming of the exhaust, felt the powerful engine respond to his silent command, and fancied himself God. The whole world was rolling away beneath those greedy wheels. Nothing could catch him.

"How do you like it, kid?" said Roy Farrell, seated beside him. "They don't make 'em any faster than this, you know."

"It's beautiful. Where'd you get it?"

Ralph Moss laughed from the back seat. Virgil heard him shift the shotgun on his knees. "We bought it. Can you believe it? Tell 'im Roy."

Farrell nodded his assent. "A guy in Oklahoma City had it. He needed money, so I offered him four thousand. He took it."

"Four grand?" repeated the driver incredulously. "For a La Salle?"

"He wasn't too happy about it."

Virgil shook his head and smiled. These bank robbers knew how to live.

Farrell reached over the back seat. "Give me that road map. I want to see where we are."

Floyd handed him the map. He rattled it and spread it across his knees. "Dawes. Let's see . . . here it is." He planted a finger on the northeast section of Oklahoma. Then he folded the map and laid it on the seat beside him. "Three miles, kid. Three miles to paradise."

Or hell, thought Virgil facetiously, and laid a hand on the heavy lump in the pocket of his new jacket.

Constable Ed Fellows had been the law in Dawes since 1887. Before that, he had been the sheriff's deputy, and before that, the stable boy. He had once replaced a shoe that had been thrown by outlaw Ford Harper's horse; four years later, duty had forced him to shoot Harper.

Now, at age sixty-six, he was still a formidable sight, for he stood six-foot-five in his knee-length trooper's boots, and, though he was stooped and had grown a slight paunch, was otherwise built like Red Grange, raw-boned and sinewy. His face was long and tanned and bony, his hair bleached white by the merciless sun. Standing with one elbow propped up on the top of the single gasoline pump in front of Fred Benson's service station, his charcoal-gray uniform spotless, he appeared quite capable of handling any emergency that should come to his town.

He was talking with Benson when the big La Salle pulled up in front of the bank. The doors opened and three men got out, leaving a fourth sitting behind the wheel. Two of them were each carrying something; without his glasses the constable couldn't tell what the objects were. One of the carriers stayed outside on the sidewalk while the other two men went into the bank.

Fellows excused himself and left Fred Benson to tend to his pump while he checked out the automobile. Part of it was healthy curiosity: he had never seen a La Salle close up.

Virgil sat peacefully behind the wheel, listening to the engine's full-throated idle. He glanced over at Floyd Moss, in the doorway of the high old brick building that was the Dawes bank. Standing there, holding a sawed-off double-barreled shotgun to discourage any unwanted visitors, he didn't look much like an Oklahoma plowboy anymore.

There wasn't much to see in Dawes, as Virgil found out when he looked it over through the La Salle's windshield. A small bakery stood next to the bank, and another door in the same building led to a general store. Beyond that, a department store rose three stories into the air, the top floor of which was boarded up and still showed signs of an ancient fire in the scorched bricks above the windows. A sign advertising its annual sale hung at a dilapidated angle across the front of the building. It had obviously been up there over a year. On the opposite side of the partially paved street stood a pair of frame buildings, one a boarding house and the other a private residence. A single-pump filling station faced the bank, billing itself FRED'S SUPER SERVICE. Virgil jumped when he spotted the man in uniform approaching. He shot a glance at Floyd. The straw-headed hick wasn't looking in the right direction.

The man in uniform had reached the car and was circling around toward Virgil's side. He was wearing a gun. Virgil hit the horn hard. Roy Farrell and Ralph Moss were just coming out of the bank when the horn sounded. Farrell had a .45 automatic pistol in one hand and a big burlap sack in the other. Ralph had a shotgun. They noticed the constable right away.

Ed Fellows froze at the sound of the horn. He whirled to face the robbers, bringing his thumb down on the leather flap of his holster at the same time. He never got it open. Ralph shoved the shotgun into the constable's midsection and fired. The top half of Fellows body twisted almost all the way around and a huge slop of blood splattered over the side of the La Salle. He was lifted off his feet, his uniform cap flew off, and he landed in a heap on the edge of the sidewalk. His cap hit on its edge and rolled all the way across the street and into the filling station.

Farrell was on the other side of the car and had the door open by the time the man landed. "Gun it!" he hollered, just as the Moss brothers catapulted themselves into the back seat, rocking the La Salle on its axles. Virgil let out the clutch and stomped down on the accelerator. The car shot forward in an explosion of exhaust and flying gravel. In a few seconds the town was behind them, growing smaller in the rear-view mirror as they roared northward.

"Son of a bitch!" exclaimed Ralph Moss in the back seat. "The bastard was going for his gun! I didn't want to shoot him. Son of a bitch!"

"Forget him," said Farrell, who had opened the sack and was pulling out thick sheaves of bills. "Look at this! There must be over twenty grand in this bag. What a haul!"

Virgil was on the edge of his seat as he wound the car around a treacherous bend in the road. His face was flushed and his heart was pounding against his chest. He liked robbing banks.

The roar of Ralph Moss' shotgun still echoed up and down the street when the denizens of Dawes came out into the sunlight. Fred Benson was the first to reach the body. He tried to turn it over, felt something warm and wet, and stood up. Then he was violently sick.

FARRELL GANG IN NEW HOLDUP!
Constable Killed in Raid on Dawes Bank.

Beneath the black headline were pictures of Roy Farrell and Ralph and Floyd Moss, front and profile. A large black question mark occupied a fourth square. Nobody had gotten a clear look at the man behind the wheel. Floyd, seated at the dining room table with the newspaper spread out before him, turned the pages slowly. "Can you believe it?" he said. "I never thought we was worth a whole god-damn special edition! If that don't beat all!"

"Who's that?" Virgil, looking over Floyd's shoulder, pointed at a blowup covering half of page six. It was a full-length shot of a mustachioed young man holding a rifle propped up on its butt. He was dressed in deerskins and a ten-gallon hat and sported two pistols in his low-slung holsters. A silver star gleamed on his chest.

Floyd read the caption below the picture. "'Ed Fellows in 1890.' Hey, that's the guy we killed!"

"You mean the guy Ralph killed." Farrell, sitting opposite Floyd, was counting bills onto the table. He looked grim.

"We're in on it just as much as Ralph," said Floyd, looking up.

Farrell ignored him, shaking his head regretfully. 'All those headlines. I don't like it. I didn't figure on attracting all this attention when I planned this job."

"Ralph planned it."

"That's right. Which makes him responsible for this whole mess." He stood up and turned to the window, looking out on Miami. "Can't you see we're crippled as long as those pictures are being circulated? We're trapped here, damn it! Trapped!"

Floyd shrugged. "So we lay low. We got enough dough."

"How much have we got?" asked Virgil, looking at the back of Farrell's head.

"I don't know. I haven't finished counting. Over eleven thousand."

"Eleven!" Virgil's voice was shrill. "You said twenty!"

"That was before I started counting." Farrell went back to the table and picked up a bundle of notes which he had laid to one side. "This stuff is mostly securities. Bonds and stuff. To us, worthless." He tossed the bundle across the table. It landed with a thump in front of Virgil. "What are we gonna do with those, hock 'em?"

Virgil fingered the notes idly. He was thinking.

Ralph came downstairs and into the dining room. He was wearing a heavy hunting shirt with the sleeves rolled up to the elbows. The back was crisscrossed with dark bands left by his suspenders while the sun had faded the rest of the shirt. His face looked ashen. He grunted when he saw the newspaper and slumped heavily into the high-backed chair in front of the telephone desk. "Crazy son-of-a-bitch constable," he muttered. "I never had to kill nobody before. Why the hell did he do it?" The others ignored him.

"What's all this about laying low?" said Virgil, leaning forward on the table. "Why don't we hit somewhere else, right now, when nobody's expecting it?"

Farrell looked pained. "Now? With our mugs all over every paper in the state? Come off it, kid!"

"No! Can't you see what all this means? It means that the next time the Farrell gang walks into a bank, people are going to stop and listen. Have you ever had trouble getting somebody to hand over the money?"

"Sometimes." The gang leader shrugged. "Now and then some teller gets the idea he's Doug Fairbanks and refuses to go along. It slows us up, but they hand over the money soon enough."

Virgil snatched the newspaper from Floyd's hands and held it up. "Well, after they read this, there won't be a soul this side of hell who'll hesitate to do what you tell him. Once they know you're ready to kill, they'll bust their asses to fill up your little burlap sack. This story is the making of us!"

"Nobody woulda got hurt if he'd just sat back," Ralph muttered from the corner. He studied the plank floor between his feet morosely.

Farrell looked from Ralph's worried face to his brother's blank one, then came back to the disturbing light in Virgil's eyes, and wondered what the hell had happened to his perfect gang.

The big official car came to a halt by the side of the highway. An Oklahoma state trooper unfolded himself from behind the wheel and climbed down the steep bank to where the long limousine sat, partially hidden by thick underbrush. Its purple finish gleamed in the late afternoon sunlight. He recognized the car as the one described in the flyer he had received two days previously, and wondered which of the nearby Tulsa banks would be robbed before he could get back to headquarters.

Meanwhile, four men were leaving a bank in Clarksville, thirty miles away, with forty thousand dollars in a burlap sack.

Chapter Six

"For me?" Hazel stared at the broad, flat box in the printer's ink-stained hands. It was wrapped in red-and-white-striped paper, and sported a green ribbon tied in a bow at the top.

The old printer nodded. "Yes, ma'am." He had to shout to make himself heard over the clattering of the big press in the center of the shop. "Fellow brought it this morning." He handed her the box.

"What did he look like?"

The printer made a sign that he couldn't hear.

"Never mind," she shouted, and, with a little wave of parting, headed for the sturdy wooden stairway that led to the second story. Once there, she juggled the gaily wrapped box underneath one arm and took her apartment key from the plaster strip above the door. She unlocked it and went in.

The setting sun showed brightly through the tall window in the opposite wall as she lugged the package over to the Victrola and set it on top. She removed her hat and gloves, threw them along with her purse onto the low easy chair beside the phonograph, and attacked the package.

The tissue paper inside the box parted to reveal the satiny folds of a bright green evening gown. She gasped in awe and reached out to touch it. The material ran through her fingers like water.

"It goes with your eyes." The voice, coming from behind her, was deliciously familiar. She turned. Virgil, resplendent in black and white pin-striped suit and patterned tie, was leaning in the bedroom doorway, grinning. He wore a gray felt hat tilted rakishly back on his head.

Hazel launched herself into his arms and kissed him hard. "It's been months," she chided, when they came up for air.

"I know," said Virgil, tossing his hat so that it landed on top of the dress. "Thought I'd bring you the frock as a peace offering. Like it?"

"It's the most beautiful thing I've ever seen." She pecked him on the cheek.

"Not too bright?"

"You said it goes with my eyes."

"The size should be right, at least. I got it from your mother."

"My mother!" She drew away to look at him. "My mother hates you, and you know it. She'd never talk to you."

Virgil grinned even broader. "She didn't, really. She thought she was talking to your dressmaker, who called her by mistake."

"You're really deceitful, aren't you?" She snuggled up to him. After a moment, she said, "I wish I had someplace to wear the gown."

This time it was he who drew away. He looked down at her. "Now, what kind of cad would send you a dress without giving you a chance to wear it?"

Hazel's face lit up. "Do you mean what I think you mean?"

He slapped her on the rump. "Put it on!"

She had the package under her arm and had fled into the bedroom almost before he could get out of the way. "And hurry it up!" he said as she closed the door. "The theaters in Oklahoma City don't hold their curtains for nobody!"

Louis Armstrong was halfway through "New Orleans Stomp" on the Victrola when Hazel came out of the bedroom. Virgil turned to face her and smiled slowly. "Oh, baby," he said in a hushed voice, "you're Garbo all over."

She blushed, but that was exactly what she wanted him to think. Her shining black hair was pinned up high, so that her green earrings were visible. She wore very little make-up, but what she did use lengthened her lashes to supernatural proportions and, she thought, put just the right touch of ruddiness to her cheeks. The dress was sleeveless and extremely low cut. Her full breasts pushed against the material and pulled it taut across the front, leaving a deep cleavage much more sensuous than that allowed on the screen. She held a white clutch purse in one white-gloved hand to complete the effect.

Virgil moved in and kissed her, lips parted. She pushed him away, gently. "Just a second," she said.

"I surely don't intend to go out hitchhiking in this outfit. Oklahoma City's too long a way to go in the back of a produce truck."

"First I'm a cad, now I'm a pauper." Virgil went over to the window and drew the curtain aside with a flourish. "Look down, my love, on the chariot of your dreams."

Hazel approached the window and looked down into the street. There, its glossy black finish icy in the glare of a streetlamp, sat a brand-new Marmon roadster. It had wire wheels and a set of white-sidewalled tires, the fifth of which was mounted on the right-hand running board. The top was down, revealing its white leather upholstery. Hazel let out a long sigh.

"Better than hitchhiking?" prompted Virgil.

She nodded. "Better than hitchhiking."

Virgil put his arm around her and escorted her toward the door. "I seem to remember saying something about coming back in style," he said, turning off the light behind him. "Well, a Ballard never breaks a promise." He closed the door, leaving the apartment in darkness.

"Meet Ron McCoy. He's our new wheel man." Farrell stood aside so that the two could get a good look at each other.

Virgil studied the kid through narrowed eyes. He was wearing a blue jacket over a brown turtleneck sweater, both new. His auburn hair had been combed carefully back and parted in the middle, Valentino-style, and his face was peppered with acne. He chewed eagerly at a wad of gum. "Pleased to meetcha, Mr. Ballard," said the boy, holding out his hand.

Virgil ignored the gesture. "What is this?" he said. "Some kind of joke?"

"Not at all." Farrell draped his arm over the boy's shoulders. "Ron, here, used to drive an ambulance in Tulsa. He can thread his way through traffic like a hopped-up seamstress. Am I right, Ron?"

The boy grinned. "Hell, I can handle anything that rolls. Just point me to the wheels, that's all I ask."

Virgil looked at Farrell, than at each of the Moss brothers, who were standing behind the gang leader, grinning from ear to ear. The kid sounded so much like Virgil on his first day with the gang that he couldn't be sure whether they were putting him on or not. "You unsatisfied with my work?"

The other three burst into laughter. The McCoy kid looked at them and smiled, as if not sure what was going on. Virgil's face grew hot. "What's so damn funny?" he demanded.

Farrell rubbed his face to clear it of mirth. "Jesus, but you're a sensitive son of a bitch," he said. "Don't you even know when you're being promoted?"

"Promoted." Virgil glanced at Ralph. "That true?"

Ralph was choking with suppressed laughter. "That's right," he finally managed to croak. "From now on, Virgie-boy, you're goin' into the bank with us!"

"In the bank? You mean it?"

"You can handle a gun," said Farrell, smiling "I saw that in Okmulgee, when you fired a shot over that bank guard's head. Just grazed the top of his cap. That was no accident. Anyway, I figure anybody who can throw lead like that doesn't belong behind the wheel."

Virgil grinned. "Ron, is it?" He thrust a hand toward the boy. "Welcome to the Farrell gang."

McCoy accepted the handshake. "Thanks a lot, Mr. Ballard. You won't regret it."

"That's settled, then." Farrell went over to the dining room table, where a crisp new road map had been spread out across the top. "Boys," he said, "this is gonna be our new base of operations." He traced a large circle with his finger on the southwestern corner of Oklahoma.

"We're moving?" asked Floyd. "Why?"

"Things are getting too hot around Miami. A few more bank jobs in this area and we'll lose our protection. Besides, we need mobility. No more of this setting up in one place. Too risky."

"We're on the run." Virgil eyed him savagely.

Farrell raised his eyes to Virgil's. "Not at all. We're just shifting to another part of the state." He focussed his concentration back on the map. "From here on in, we're living out of a suitcase."

Apache, Oklahoma.

The head cashier had his back turned when the big Studebaker pulled up in front of the bank's window, so he didn't see the four men get out and head for the door. He was turning back to his customer when somebody gasped. He looked up.

One of the men, a big, towheaded farmboy-type, remained outside while the other three entered the bank. The first through the door was an Indian, wearing a sharp double-breasted suit and a well-trimmed black moustache. He had a pistol in his hand. Just behind him, a short bulldog of a man came in carrying a shotgun. His eyes swept the room and came to rest on the teller. The third was a young fellow, well-dressed and innocent-looking in spite of the big Luger he kept trained on the cashier's mid-section. They swiftly crossed the waxed tile floor and stopped before the head cashier's cage. The customer who had been standing there drifted away, hands in the air.

"All right," said the Indian calmly, "this is just what you think it is, folks. We're gonna attend to our business and leave, and nobody's gonna get hurt . . . as long as nothing unexpected happens."

There was a great silence in the room. The five or six customers who had been lined up at the tellers' windows raised their hands slowly without waiting to be told. The head cashier saw out of the corner of his eye that the other two bank employees had done the same. Then he raised his own hands, pausing only to resettle his spectacles on his prominent nose.

"Not you," said the Indian, twitching the muzzle of his pistol. "You're gonna need your hands." He unfolded the small burlap sack he'd been carrying beneath his arm and opened it. "Fill 'er up."

The cashier slid open his cash drawer and began loading bundles of bills into the sack. He couldn't resist the urge to count them mentally as they disappeared down the burlap mouth. His salary for the previous year went by the first fifteen seconds.

One of the bank's customers, a woman, dropped

her purse and it hit the floor with a thump. The innocent-looking young man whirled at the sound and thrust his Luger in the woman's direction. His finger was prevented from squeezing the trigger when the Indian dropped his sack and grabbed his partner's wrist. "Calm down!" he snapped.

The cashier hit the alarm button with his foot. The bell above the door began clanging. Twisting free of the Indian's grip, the young man aimed his Luger at the cashier, seemed to think better of it, wheeled, and shot the bell. It exploded in a cloud of torn metal and went on ringing in a different key.

"Let's clear the hell out!". The Indian snatched up the half-full sack and ran out the door on the heels of his companions. The Studebaker was rolling by the time they had the doors open. In the next moment it was gone, its passing marked by a swiftly settling cloud of red dust.

"I should've plugged that sonuvabitch cashier the minute we walked in." Virgil, in shirtsleeves and vest, stared down at the moonlight rippling across the surface of Lake Lawtonka. A moth fluttered and banged at the screen door a few inches in front of his face, struggling to get near the light.

Ralph, slouched in an overstuffed chair beneath a wrought iron floor lamp, grunted above his copy of the *Literary Digest*. "I wish to hell you'd quit grousing," he said. "There ain't nobody around to hear it anyways." He turned the page and admired a full-length shot of Arnie Rothstein.

"What in God's name did Roy go to Elgin for anyway, this time of night?"

"Movie. 'The Mark of Zorro.' Doug Fairbanks." Ralph made a parrying motion with his right hand, swinging an imaginary sword. "Ron was driving."

The moth was still clinging to the screen, fascinated by the light.

"Eight thousand goddamn dollars. We did better than that in Dawes."

Ralph wasn't listening. Arnie Rothstein. Ten million dollars a year.

"The trouble with these jerk bank tellers, they don't respect guns."

"Shut up. Floyd's trying' to sleep."

"Guns aren't just for looks. We got to teach them that. What we got to do, we got to start using 'em, like in Dawes." Virgil felt the weight of his Luger pulling against the shoulder holster beneath his vest. He had bought the rig on the way across the state, from a high-class sporting goods store outside of Guthrie, and had not yet stopped congratulating himself on the purchase. It felt good.

"The next time we walk into a bank," he said, "we got to kill somebody." He reached out and crushed the moth.

Farrell, seated on the end of the wooden dock, finished baiting his hook and dropped the line into the water. The red-and-white bobber danced twice on the metallic surface and sat still.

Ralph Moss watched it for a few seconds, then directed his attention back to his boss. He was standing above Farrell, hands thrust deep into his pockets. "We got to do something about Virgil," he said at last.

"I know." The gang leader fished a cigarette and lighter from an inside pocket of his jacket, placed the cigarette between his lips, and lit it one-handed. "What else did he say?"

Ralph shrugged. "That was it. He says, 'We got to kill somebody,' and goes upstairs. Nothin' else."

"Think he meant it?"

"He meant it, all right. Virgil don't joke much."

"Yeah." The bobber jiggled and returned to its original position. A nibble. "He almost shot that dame back in Apache."

"He would of, too, if you hadn't stopped him. That boy's bad news, Roy. We can't afford to have him around no more."

"That's your lookout. You hired him, remember?"

Ralph sighed heavily. "I was afraid you'd say that." He watched a duck come in low over the water and brake to a standstill on the surface, like a seaplane. "Okay, I'll tell him he's got to go."

"You don't have to tell me nothin'!"

Ralph turned. He heard the dock creak and knew Farrell had done the same. Virgil, hatless, his jacket unbuttoned, was standing on the bank at the other end of the dock. His face was a mask of fury. "You four-for-a-quarter sons of bitches," he hissed.

"How long you been standing there?" Ralph demanded.

"Long enough." Virgil strode across the dock, drew back his fist, and smashed Ralph square in the face. The solid Oklahoman staggered backward, scrambling to keep from losing his balance and toppling into the clear water. He succeeded, then charged toward Virgil, snorting like a mad bull.

"Hold it!" Farrell reached out and took hold of Ralph's ankle. His momentum carried him forward and he pitched facedown onto the dock. "Knock it off!" The gang leader indicated the peaceful cottages on the other side of the lake. "You want somebody to complain and call the law down on us?"

Ralph, who had climbed to his hands and knees, relaxed somewhat. He got to his feet and brushed the dust off his trousers.

Virgil's face was flushed. "You bastards can worry about the law by yourselves from here on in. I'm clearing out." He wheeled and headed back toward the cottage.

"What are you gonna do?" Farrell's voice carried across the lake and came back. He was resting on one hip on the end of the dock, watching the young man's progress up the grassy hill.

Virgil stopped and turned, looking down at the two figures on the dock. "Read the papers," he shouted. "You'll find out." He hesitated a moment longer, then spun on his heel and resumed his journey toward the house and the black roadster parked before the garage.

Part II

Escapee

The bloodhounds strain at their leashes, baying around the legs of Oklahoma City Sheriff Roger McCracken. He is a big man, a barrel balanced solidly upon a pair of long and incongruously lanky legs, his square head surmounted by a broad-brimmed approximation of a Western hat. His uniform consists of tan breeches stuffed into the tops of a battered pair of half boots and a heavy black jacket zipped halfway up the front with a star insignia on the upper left sleeve. He reaches down, grabs a thick fold of loose dog flesh, and shakes it. "Best damn hounds on this side of Tulsa."

"Where the hell have you been?" Farnum, a faceless shadow in the mouth of the alley, fingers the butt of his machine gun nervously. "He could be in Missouri by now."

The sheriff squints distastefully at the trench-coated figure before him and spits onto the invisible pavement. "Fuck you. I had to wake up the guy in charge before I could get the dogs."

Farnum ignores the sheriff's belligerence. "Let's get going." He leads the way out into the street, where the glow of a number of flashlights points out the locations of the various lawmen. The drizzling rain splatters loudly against the sidewalks and pavement. A few brave souls, awakened by the gunfire of a few minutes before and the persistent baying of the hounds, have ventured out of their doors, but they remain in the shelter of their porches, out of the way.

"Jake! Take these things off my hands, will you?"

The lanky deputy sheriff trots over to relieve his superior of the noisy dogs. He is either chewing a fresh wad of gum or is still working at the old piece. Another deputy, who has been holding Sheriff McCracken's shotgun, hands the weapon back to the lawman.

"All right," snaps Farnum. "We'll stick with this street. Sheriff, take your men and search the alleys and side streets. Leave the dogs with us."

The sheriff glares at Farnum. In the peripheral illumination afforded by the flashlights, the special agent's ruddy face is hard and tense. His mind is clearly concerned with his prey and nothing else. The sheriff nods his assent and turns away, signaling his deputies to follow him.

The hounds, their leashes now held by a special agent, fall silent, sniffing the air. They get the scent and lunge forward, baying and snapping as the agent scrambles to keep up with them.

Sheriff McCracken watches as the trench-coated agents move on in the hounds' path. Then he turns and leads the way into a narrow alley. Jake, the gangling deputy, follows his superior's broad back, along with the other men in uniform. Soon the street is silent.

Chapter Seven

December 24, 1926.

The thick record wobbled around and around inside the portable crank-up phonograph, occasionally taking time out between scratches to allow Ruth Etting's voice to come through, warbling "Silent Night." George Shipman, proprietor of "Shipman's, the most well-equipped drugstore in Okmulgee," was working late to fill a prescription for his wife's mother. Christmas or not, people still got sick. He finished the last few capsules and slid them into a sterile glass bottle, funneling them through the round neck via a narrow slip of white paper.

Outside the plate-glass window, tiny flakes of snow swarmed and swirled through the night air, flashing like fireflies as they caught and reflected the light from inside the store. Freezing winds whined around the corners of the brick building, making Shipman doubly grateful for the warmth emanating from the little olive-drab furnace in the corner behind the counter. It cheered him to look up from his work and see the hearty little flame glowing through the thick glass window in the side of the furnace and reflecting the colorful ornaments on the small Christmas tree standing on the nearby display table. It made the holiday seem worthwhile.

He wiped the top of the bottle with the slip of paper and shoved in the stopper. Then he transferred the tiny container to the pocket of his white coat. Behind him, the phonograph had stuck and the record went on, over and over: "Tender and, tender and, tender and —" Shipman lifted the arm and set it down again closer to the center of the disk. It resumed playing.

He was turning back to the counter when the bell above the door jangled and somebody came in, bringing a gust of icy wind in with him. The stranger was a tall, broad-shouldered fellow, well dressed in a suit and heavy topcoat that hung to his knees. Shipman was unable to see the man's face beneath the broad-brimmed hat he had pulled low over his eyes. He strode down the aisle, brushed past a cardboard cutout of Santa Claus set up to display a table of cosmetics, and stopped before the counter.

The proprietor could now see his customer's face in the light of the shaded lamp that hung from the ceiling. It was a young face, freckled slightly from the Oklahoma sun, and set off by a pair of cool blue eyes that regarded Shipman steadfastly. His nose was finely structured, so much so that, from the front, one could only make out the slight depression above the bridge and the contours of the well-formed nostrils, while the rest of it disappeared against the background of the evenly tanned face. Only the mouth, the wide, thin-lipped mouth, set as it was, served to suggest the possible presence of a violent temperament. It was a cruel slash in what was otherwise a peaceful visage. Shipman also noticed a few wisps of sun-bleached hair which the somber hat had been powerless to imprison. Obviously a farm boy who had made good in the city.

"Merry Christmas, sir," the druggist said smiling. "Is there something I can do for you?"

"Yeah." The young man brought an ugly, foreign-looking automatic pistol from his coat pocket and aimed it at him, "Reach."

Shipman's eyes flitted to the gun, then back to the stranger's face. He smiled uncertainly. "Why — what kind of a Christmas joke is this?"

"I said reach!" The man's voice was savage. He brought the gun up higher.

The druggist was puzzled. Was this for real? Surely no Christian would consider robbing his fellow man on Christmas Eve! He hesitated, searching the stranger's face for some sign that he was joking. Then the man fired.

Shipman heard the pistol roar and saw the flames leap from the barrel before he felt anything. Then something red hot drilled into his insides. He gasped and doubled over, feeling the warm blood flow between and over the fingers he had clapped over the wound. He sank to his knees and toppled sideways to the well-swept floor, hearing the rattle of the stranger's hand in the drawer of the cash register. Footsteps hurried away, the little bell jangled, and the door banged shut. Then came darkness.

Above his head, the record had stuck again. It kept repeating, "Sleep, sleep, sleep."

Virgil wound the second-hand Buick around the corner and into Tulsa's business district. He liked the spacious sedan, but every time he put his foot down on the accelerator, he missed the little Marmon roadster he had been forced to leave behind in Stillwater. If he had plugged that jerk in Chickasha who had seen him escape from the Farmer's Bank & Trust job in the little black bomb, he would still be using it. It was the all-points bulletin put out by the Stillwater police that had turned the trick; he'd barely had time to ditch it and buy the Buick before every damn cop in town had zeroed in on his trail. But he couldn't complain about the used heap, for it had been in his possession over a year without incident. He was glad nobody had seen him leaving the drugstore back in Okmulgee, or he would have to give up this one, too.

It was January, 1927, the dawn of a new year, but Tulsa hadn't changed. Bigger, perhaps, than when he had last seen it, and noisier; Virgil didn't notice it. The multi-laned streets were no less confusing than they had ever been, and the skyscrapers still reached high into the air on both sides, making a tunnel of the broad avenue. A few buildings had been added since his last visit, their clean new facades contrasting sharply against the drab grays and browns of the edifices around them. Not far away, construction was under way on still newer buildings. Bricks and lumber and equipment and bags of cement were piled in stacks in the center of vacant lots and near half-finished foundations, some of the stacks spilling over onto the sidewalks. Some rich bastards showing off their millions, thought Virgil, and turned the corner. The big business boom had infected everbody. Including bank robbers.

There were numerous hotels in the area , any one of which would have been suitable for Virgil, had it not been for their rates. It had been a long time since his last big score, and he had long since gone through his cut from the Farrell days. He was searching for a more rundown building, the kind that advertised low rates. Something between a flophouse and the Savoy. With this in mind, he guided the car away from the downtown area and toward the poorer section of Tulsa.

It was fortunate for Officer William Creiderman that he was standing near a telephone booth when the blue Buick came down his street. He had just stepped out the door of the Atlas Cafe, his stomach comfortably packed full of doughnuts, and was frowning at the coffee spots on the front of his blue uniform tunic when the sound of tires squeaking on the wet pavement made him look up. He eyed the car, looked up at the driver, and blinked.

He had seen that profile just a few minutes before, in the center of a wanted circular his station had received that morning. He took a copy of that circular from his pocket and studied it. He had been right. The same young face, without the hat, peered out at him from beneath the familiar WANTED legend. The man's name was spelled out underneath the pictures, but that was of no importance to Creiderman. He shoved the circular back into his pocket and stepped into the phone booth, dialing as he watched the big sedan recede into the distance.

Virgil could read the vertical sign through the window of the shabby lobby: THE WAYFARER MOTEL. Most of the electric bulbs in the sign had been smashed, leaving three at the top and two at the bottom to cast a ghostly glow over the black letters. His car was parked in the street below and across from the sign, evaporating into the swiftly gathering dusk. He wondered if it would be safe in this neighborhood.

He struck the crusty bell impatiently with the heel of his hand. A tiny cloud of dust rose from the battered desk as he did so, sliding and settling into a fan-shaped design across the blotter. It was another minute before the fat little man appeared in the doorway of the room behind the desk, his bald pate shining sickly green in the light of the shaded bulb that hung from the ceiling. He wore a white shirt, yellowed at the collar, and a neutral-colored vest that had worn fuzzy around the seams and buttons. He reached the desk and stood looking up at Virgil expectantly.

"How about a room?" said Virgil.

The man grunted something unintelligible and flipped open the thick book on the counter. He found a page that was half filled with scrawled signatures and turned the book toward the customer, at the same time holding out a fountain pen. Virgil took it and scribbled the name "Oscar Miller" across the first blank space.

"The pen," the clerk reminded him mildly.

Virgil, who had been in the process of absent-mindedly slipping the fountain pen into his jacket pocket, hesitated and returned it to the clerk's outstretched hand. The little man turned and unhooked a tagged key from the board behind the counter, but held it back instead of handing it over. "That'll be two bucks for the day — in advance."

The customer reached inside his jacket and produced his billfold, from which he extracted two bills, and laid them in the clerk's palm. They disappeared immediately and the key was extended. Virgil grasped it and dropped it into his side pocket. "I'll get my luggage."

He crossed the dusty-tile floor, opened the door and went out. A blast of cold air greeted him as he stepped onto the sidewalk and headed for his car, causing him to turn up the collar of his jacket.

Night had descended while he was inside the building, its inky blackness creeping up to the circle of lamplight that now surrounded the Buick and crouching inside it. The overcast sky effectively concealed the moon and stars so that the lighted windows of the skyscrapers on both sides of the street seemed to be floating against a background of deep ebony. It was a typical winter night in Tulsa, thought Virgil as he pulled open the door on the driver's side and slid in behind the wheel.

There was a movement in the back seat and something hard was placed against the base of his skull.

Virgil stiffened and glanced up at the rear-view mirror, but the shadows in the back seat were too dense for him to see who it was. What he did see were three men in blue uniforms converging on the car, their exposed revolvers glinting in the light of the street lamp. Virgil thought about the Luger in his shoulder holster, then felt the prodding of the other gun against the back of his neck, and relaxed.

"Now, just behave yourself and we'll all live longer," hissed a voice behind him.

Chapter Eight

"Will the defendant please rise."

Virgil obeyed the judge's flat command, rising unsteadily to his feet. The jury's verdict still rang in his head. His forehead felt cold and damp.

The judge cleared his throat. "Virgil Ballard, you have been found guilty of murder in the first degree. I have no choice but to sentence you to prison for the rest of your natural life. This court is adjourned." He rapped his gavel sharply on the bench and left the room.

There was a tense silence following the statement, broken only by the rush of reporters through the big double doors at the back of the courtroom. Virgil stood staring at the spot where the judge's fleshy face had been, half expecting the entire nightmare to dissolve beneath the clamor of some celestial alarm clock. It didn't.

The court-appointed lawyer got to his feet and placed a fatherly hand on Virgil's shoulder. "I'm sorry, kid," he murmured. "It was the best I could get you. The D.A. was pushing for the chair."

"Shut up." Virgil kept his eyes on the bench.

The lawyer nodded gravely. "I understand."

Hazel didn't move from her seat for a long time after sentence had been passed. She knew that she should be with Virgil, that she should comfort him, tell him she'd wait for him, but she couldn't. She just sat there, staring at his back, and wishing she hadn't come. The spectators began filing out of the courtroom, some of them stealing glances at her as they went by and whispering to their companions. She didn't pay any attention to them. She just kept watching Virgil, her eyes following him as the two policemen took him gently but firmly by the arms and escorted him down the aisle and out the door. Then she wept.

"Ballard?" The warden looked up at Hazel, taking in her yellow silk turban, narrow skirt, high-heeled pumps, and, because he was human, lingered a moment on her shapely legs, then brought his gaze back up to fix her large green eyes. "You're his wife?"

"His fiancee," lied Hazel. She had heard that the Oklahoma State Prison at McAlester only allowed inmates to be visited by their attorneys and members of their families. While the authorities' records would show that Virgil had no wife, she hoped they would make an exception for his "future intended." She looked at the warden hopefully.

The gleam of admiration vanished from the middle-aged official's eyes, to be replaced by a paternal sobriety in his heavy knitted brows and down-turned mouth. "I'd advise you to forget him, miss. It will be a very long time before he sees the light of day, if ever. He's in for life, you know."

"Yes, I know. Could I see him?"

"That would be highly irregular. The regulations of this penitentiary specifically state that a prisoner may only receive visits, as well as correspondence, from the members of his immediate family. And, of course, from his attorney. I seldom make exceptions in this regard."

Hazel was growing impatient. "The only reason that I am not a member of Virgil Ballard's family is because he was arrested before we could be married. Are you going to forbid me to see the man I love on such a technicality?" She stared down at him from above the desk, her eyes flashing hostility.

"As I said, it would be highly irregular." The white-haired official lapsed into silence for a long moment, during which he appeared to be battling with himself. Finally his face cleared and he looked up at Hazel. "Very well, miss. I'll let you talk to him. But only for a few minutes." With that, he rose from his seat, crossed to the connecting door between his office and the adjoining one, and opened it. "Would you come in here, Rodriguez?"

A moment later, a tall, dark-complexioned guard, whom Hazel had seen earlier in the outer office, came in, wearing a well-pressed gray uniform that looked new. He closed the door behind him and glanced expectantly from Hazel to the warden.

"Show this lady into the receiving room," the warden directed him, "and have inmate Ballard sent there too."

"Yes, sir." The young guard held open the door and made a polite gesture that meant Hazel should go first. Then he followed her out of the room.

The receiving room, at the end of a dingy green corridor several floors below the warden's office, was a large, high-ceilinged room, divided by a long table that stretched from one side of the room to the other. A wire grid ran down the center of this table, and a row of straight-backed wooden chairs were drawn up on each side, some of them occupied. The guard led her to one of these and she sat down. "He'll be here in a moment, miss," he said quietly, and left.

The room buzzed with voices. Convicts in somber gray work clothes engaged in low conversations with their wives and lawyers, obviously attempting to keep beyond earshot of the placid-faced guards who stood nearby, listening. The electric lights were off, so that the only illumination came from the gray, diffused sunlight that filtered in soft beams through the barred windows near the lofty ceiling. The effect was depressing, the drab forms of caged men huddling in half shadow and attempting to establish some link with the lighted world beyond the walls sparking a sobering reaction in Hazel.

She rummaged through her purse, located her compact, and began repairing her make-up. The face in the tiny mirror looked about the same as it had when Virgil had last seen it, the night he had taken her to the theater in Oklahoma City, but she wasn't sure. Would he like the paler shade of lipstick she had adopted, or the fullness in her cheeks that had replaced the Garbo-like hollows? At least the warden had seemed to appreciate her looks. But then, he was an old man. It was likely that he would find any young woman attractive. But would Virgil? She was considering these questions when the dark young guard appeared in the mirror and took his place beside the door. She snapped the compact shut and looked up. Virgil was standing on the other side of the table, gazing down at her.

He was wearing a gray linen uniform with the number 28715 stencilled across a patch on his shirt pocket. For a moment, Hazel was reminded of the days when gray work clothes were the only kind of apparel Virgil owned. But one look at the hard lines in his face was enough to wipe away any resemblance between this Virgil and the old Virgil. This man was a caged animal.

The guard who had escorted him to the receiving room remained beside the door, his face a blank mask. Virgil slid out his chair and sat down opposite his visitor.

"Hello, Hazel." The greeting was flat and unemotional.

Hazel smiled uncertainly. "Hello, Virgil. You look healthy." Actually, his complexion was sallow and he looked quite ill.

He ignored the observation. "I saw you at the trial. You didn't come over to where I was sitting."

"I was — afraid." She lowered her eyes for an instant, then brought them back to his. "I thought you didn't want to see me."

Virgil didn't answer, but kept watching her face.

She went on. "You didn't come to see me for so many months. I thought you had somebody else. That I didn't mean anything to you anymore."

"You're a fool." There was a faint trace of tenderness in his tone. "You're mine, no matter how long I'm gone. I thought you knew that."

"I'm yours. That's why I couldn't bring myself to speak to you at the trial. That's why I'm here now." Tears shone in her eyes. "I came to tell you that I'll be waiting when you get out."

"Don't."

Hazel blinked. A tear came free and rolled swiftly down her right cheek. "What?"

"I said, don't wait." Virgil's face was impassive. "Hazel, I'm gonna be in here for the rest of my life. I'll never come out. What good is it gonna do for you to wait?"

"Stop, Virgil! Please don't say any more."

Virgil showed no sign that he'd heard her. "I'm not making any sacrifices," he said. "I'm just trying to stop you from doing something stupid like becoming an old maid for my sake. It isn't worth it."

"Stop!"

"Find some guy and marry him. Have kids. But please don't make me feel like a heel because we can't be together. I can't live with that. Not in stir." He rose and summoned the guard who had brought him. The man in uniform came over.

Hazel stood up an instant after Virgil did, her fingers clutching the iron grid that separated them. "Virgil! Don't go!"

Virgil smiled for the first time since he entered the room, a genuine, cocky grin. "So long, Garbo."

"Virgil!" shouted Hazel, but it was too late.

There was no Ralph Moss in McAlester to occupy Virgil's time by planning great robberies. When he wasn't manning the big steam press in the prison laundry, he spent the few minutes of leisure time allowed him hanging around the inmates' barber shop. While the barber, a trustee, snipped away at his fellow convicts' locks, Virgil would sit down in the chair nearest the radio and listen.

It was a big set, one of those knob-studded metal cabinet receivers with a huge horn speaker curving up from its top like the funnel of a battleship. Virgil would cross his legs and pretend to read a magazine while in reality keeping his ear cocked toward the sounds that came from the monstrous machine. The big radio was Virgil's only link with the outside world, and he was determined to make use of that link whenever possible.

On February 14, 1929, one year and eight months after Virgil Ballard had begun his stay in McAlester, seven men were found machine-gunned to death in a garage on Chicago's North Clark Street. Within two days, it was announced over the barbershop radio that the probable instigator of the St. Valentine's Day Massacre was none other than Al Capone, and that one of the suspected killers was Fred (Killer) Burke, former Midwestern bank robber, late of the Detroit Purple Gang.

When Virgil heard this, he almost dropped the month-old copy of *Liberty* he had been pretending to read and looked up at the ugly speaker. He had met Fred Burke, back in the Farrell days. At that time, Burke had been a skinny punk who spent most of his time following Virgil wherever he went and begging the older robber to show him the big Luger "just one more time." Finally the strain of ducking the punk had gotten to be too much and Virgil had talked Farrell into giving the kid his walking papers. And now they called him "Killer." Virgil shook his head and turned to an article about Lenin.

When he wasn't sitting within earshot of the radio, Virgil was busy operating the steam press in the laundry. He had been at it so long that he had begun to take pride in his work, folding the damp gray prison uniforms just so, so that he could put a sharp professional crease right down the sleeves and along the seams, just as he had seen his mother do with a flatiron when he was a boy. He called it "the Ballard press," but only to himself. Pride in one's accomplishments behind bars was not likely to be received favorably by one's fellow inmates at McAlester. But he still felt satisfaction when he saw a hardened con walking the yard with the Ballard press prominently displayed on his uniform. Indeed, the only time he didn't dwell over the passage of time in prison was when he was swinging down the heavy top of the big press and listening with satisfaction as the steam hissed solidly out through the apertures in the side.

Doubly satisfying to him was the knowledge that his "servant," the man who carted the laundry to and from the press, had been a vice-president of multimillion dollar corporation on the outside. Unfortunately for him, some young efficiency expert had discovered that the big shot had been dipping into the till to support an extravagant mistress, and here he was. Virgil enjoyed ordering him around and read him out unmercifully whenever he dropped a load of freshly pressed uniforms, which happened often because the man suffered from arthritis. He felt superior to the older con, for one simple reason: Bank robbers were more honest than embezzlers. "You know you're being robbed when a guy pokes a gun in your ribs and demands money," Virgil told him once, "but when one of your own employees goes wrong, he can steal you blind before you realize it." The man had merely glared at him with a pained look on his face and turned away to pick up a fresh batch of uniforms.

One day in October, 1929, the ex-big shot failed to show up. When his replacement arrived, Virgil asked him casually what had happened to "John D. Rockefeller."

The ruddy-faced replacement looked at him a moment before he spoke. "He's dead."

"Dead?" Virgil was taken aback. "What happened? Did he fall off his wallet?"

"Search me," shrugged the other. "All I know is, a buddy of mine who works in the hospital says they carried him out this morning with the sheet over his face."

It wasn't until late that afternoon, when Virgil was listening to the radio in the barbershop, that he figured out what had happened. A deep-voiced announcer boomed out the news that the stock market had taken the biggest plunge in its history. It was the beginning of the crash. Then Virgil saw everything clearly. The ex-vice-president had every reason to believe that when his sentence was over he would have over a million dollars coming from his investments. Now, that hope had been dashed, along with all the others, and it had been too much. The shock had killed him.

But time passed for Virgil Ballard. The Roaring Twenties died with a whimper, and 1930 sprang upon the prison as it did everywhere else. Unemployment loomed dark in the future. Businesses died. As the stark statistics began to roll from the radio, Virgil began for the first time to feel grateful for his presence in the prison, and to look forward each morning to operating the press. He thought of himself as one of a very few who had nothing to worry about in the way of layoffs and firings.

"Busy, Virge?"

Virgil knew who it was without turning. There was only one man in the whole prison who called him by that name. He snapped off the radio and leaned back in his seat, regarding Alex Kern from beneath heavy eyelids.

Alex grinned at Virgil from his place beside him on the bench, showing off his gold tooth. He was a long, lanky lad, like Virgil, but in a city-bred way, and had a shock of dull black hair which he kept cropped close to his head around the back and temples, letting it grow full and thick on top. His sleepy eyelids would have made him look backward had it not been for his quick, cockeyed smile that so disarmed anyone upon whom he chose to train it. The combination added up to a witty and cocksure appearance. He looked more like a con man than a bank robber. From what Virgil had learned of the man's past, he knew that Kern was a combination of both.

"Does it look like I'm busy?" Virgil slipped a cigarette from his shirt pocket and lit it.

"I never can tell, you're always listening to that damn squawk box."

"So what's up?"

Kern eyed the sullen barber, who was finishing off the back of a convict's neck with his razor. "Not here. Let's go to your cell."

Virgil shook his head. "Not now, I got fifteen minutes before I go back there."

"Well, we got to go somewhere private."

"All right." Virgil got up from the bench and led the way out into the yard. The two convicts pushed through the clusters of gray-clad men who had gathered in the well-trodden area, and came to a stop in a quiet corner of the wall beneath the west tower.

"Spill it," said Virgil.

Alex glanced around furtively, looked up at the bell that would soon call them back to their cells, then returned his gaze to Virgil's freckled face. "They tell me you're a hotshot when there's a vault around."

Virgil didn't answer, but regarded him coolly.

Kern went on. "They say the same thing about me. But we're both in stir, ain't we? So we can't be such hotshots after all."

"Speak for yourself."

"Yeah. Well, have you ever thought why guys like us keep getting caught?" The reedy con didn't wait for an answer. "We keep getting caught because the cops ain't scared enough of us."

Virgil smiled for the first time, but his smile was grim. "Yeah, I noticed that. I keep expecting 'em to run away whenever I come out of a bank with a bag of money in my hand. I can't imagine why they don't."

Alex ignored the sarcasm. "We can make 'em run, you know. Or stand still. Anything we want." He looked around once again, then reached into his sweat-stained shirt and pulled out a folded sheet of thin paper, which he spread out beneath Virgil's nose.

It was a sheet torn from a magazine. It was wrinkled, and there were two notches in one edge of the page where the staples had been. But that wasn't what caught Virgil's eye. There was an illustration at the top of the sheet, a long black silhouette that somewhat resembled the others on the page, yet was different. The gun's squat buttstock was shaped much like those below it, as was the barrel, though a little shorter than the others, but there were two curved grips that were not found in any of the other rifles.

The most important difference, however, was the round piepan drum suspended from the stout barrel. It was a Thompson submachine gun, model 1928, equipped with a fifty-shot drum. The statistics beneath the picture identified it as a .45-caliber, capable of firing 1600 rounds per minute. Virgil whistled in spite of himself.

"Some gun, huh?" Alex held it under his companion's nose a moment longer, then refolded it and returned it to the inside of his shirt. "Them guys in Chicago used two of these last year in that garage."

Virgil had recovered his cool exterior. "It's a good gun. So what?"

"I know where we can get one."

It was a long time before Virgil spoke. Then he

sneered. "Good for you. How do you plan to smuggle it past the gate?"

Kern placed a hand on his arm, stopping him. "I'm not talking about now." This time it was his turn to sneer. "You think I'm idiot enough to make a break with only six months left to serve?"

"I don't know. What are you talking about?" Virgil let his arm drop.

Kern slapped his chest, rustling the sheet of paper that was folded aginst it. "I know a place where they keep a whole bunch of these meat-choppers. It won't take nothin' to break 'em out. Man, when somebody shows up with one of them under his arm, ain't nobody gonna get in his way. If you'd had one back in Tulsa, you'd be on the streets right now."

Virgil thought about that, and decided Kern was right. "Yeah. So?"

"So just imagine you and me walking into a bank and letting little old Tommy do the talking."

"You crazy? I'm in for life. Last I heard, nobody was planning to put a branch of the First National here in McAlester."

Alex Kern straightened in his seat and relaxed. "Well, now, that's where I come in."

Then the bell rang.

Chapter Nine

July 14, 1931.

Bastille Day entered McAlester Penitentiary to a
fanfare that made the celebration in Paris pale by
comparison. High-pitched sirens split the air, their
screams rising and falling like crashing waves, doubling and redoubling as other mechanical clarions
joined them. The naked stone towers came ablaze
in a sudden flare of searchlights and swayed eerily
as the white beams shifted and crossed within the
confines of the barren yard. On a less cosmic level
the shadows in the yard moved and spewed forth
uniformed guards from all over, running and shouting to each other as they brandished their freshly
unslung weapons before them. The heavy machine
guns in the towers flashed in the harsh artificial light
as their operators swung them into position and fixed

their brass sights on the illuminated area below. In the space of a few seconds, the entire heap of stone and steel had been transformed into a hunting creature.

Virgil Ballard paid no attention to the commotion as he crawled slowly and laboriously up a rope of knotted sheets and mattress covers to the top of the south wall. Once there, he rammed his heel against his homemade grabbling hook to set it deeper into the wall's ancient fissure, flung the rope to the other side, and slid down to the ground outside the prison. Then he began to run.

A guard spotted him, shouted, and swiveled his machine gun in line with Virgil's retreating back. Virgil felt the dirt hit his legs as the bullets chewed up the ground behind him and put on an extra burst of speed. In the next moment he had outrun the searchlights and the darkness swallowed him up.

The gates burst open and a massive touring car roared out through the opening, spraying gravel as it took the turn and bounded off the road, bouncing over the clotted field in pursuit of its lone prey. Virgil heard its powerful engine surging behind him and ran faster. He stumbled over the knotted clumps of weeds, tore headlong through the underbrush, and plunged into a small wooded lot. Behind him, the headlights of the touring car groped over the field like two relentless fingers, sweeping and searching for some sign of movement in the myriad shadows. Virgil veered out of the woods and headed up a grassy slope toward the ridge that etched the horizon. His blood was pounding in his ears and he felt his breath sawing in his throat when his feet clapped on the gravel road. He collapsed across the road and lay there, facedown, breathing the dust that settled slowly around him.

The surface began to vibrate and something growled in the distance, increasing in volume as it drew near. Soon it became a roar, and this was accompanied by the sound of flying gravel, then was overcome by the grind of a transmission collapsing steadily downward. Tires scraped on gravel, a car door slammed shut.

"Virge? You all right?"

Virgil rolled over on his back. He couldn't make out Alex Kern's features in the glare of the headlights, but he fancied he saw a crooked grin on his slim face.

"Hell, boy, you're just out of shape. Come on."

He hauled Virgil to his feet and helped him into the little coupe's front seat. Then he got in and hit the accelerator. The back wheels spun and the car bolted away before the lights of the big touring car showed above the ridge.

Standing in the warden's office in his uniform, the head of the Oklahoma State Police looked bigger than he was. His abnormally broad shoulders and thick torso added to the illusion by tapering smoothly into a narrow waist, itself hung with a military cartridge belt and another, distinctly unregulation belt with a broad Western buckle. In reality, during the few seconds that the warden had remained standing to greet him, the officer had been forced to look up at the older man.

Now, as the warden took his seat behind the worn desk, he indicated the small armchair in the corner.

The officer drew the chair up to the desk and sat down.

"Cigar?" The warden flipped open the carved wooden box at his elbow. The officer shook his head. The warden shrugged and lit one for himself. He held the match to the end longer than he had to, puffed furiously, then shook it out and dropped it into a brass ashtray, already littered with butts and the corpses of other matches. Then he sat back. "Well," he said, "how can I help the state police?"

"There are a few things I'd like to know," said the other quickly. He had a high, sharp voice, urgent and irritating. "First of all, how did Ballard escape?"

"That's easy enough." The warden opened his desk drawer and drew out something long and thin, which he handed to his visitor. It was a narrow strip of steel, a little over twelve inches long, with a machine-serrated edge.

"Hacksaw blade," explained the warden calmly. "Ballard used it to saw through the bars in the window of his cell. The teeth were still hot when we found it lying in the yard."

The officer examined the blade closely, turning it over in his fingers. Then he laid it on the desk. "Where'd he get it?"

"That's the embarrassing part," said the warden after a moment's hesitation. "We figure it was smuggled into the prison by Ballard's lawyer, a man by the name of Arthur Pennant."

"A lawyer?" The officer raised his eyebrows.

"Probably not, may have been an imposter. According to one of the guards, the man's description fits that of one of Alex Kern's old associates who was never apprehended. Kern's been on the streets about a year now."

"That means they're together." The officer unbuttoned his shirt pocket and withdrew a cigarette, which he lit with the aid of a battered lighter. "It also means that at least one of your guards has been bought."

The other nodded gravely. "It seems likely. Somebody had to be looking the other way when that saw was passed over the top of the grid."

The state cop hissed disgustedly through his teeth. "I don't know how you people expect us to do our job when you keep letting your prisoners escape," he said bitterly.

The warden rose to the bait. "I don't know how *you* people expect us to do *our* job when you keep giving *your* prisoners a slap on the wrist instead of a sentence." The two glared at each other across the top of the desk.

"Well, we aren't getting anywhere with this." The officer placed a palm on the desk. "Do you want your prisoner back, or not?"

The warden's face was curious. "What do you mean?"

"Virgil Ballard. According to our files, he comes from up North. Around Picher."

The warden nodded. "That's right. We have files too, you know."

"Well, *our* files show he has a girl up there. Hazel something. They haven't seen each other for four years."

Realization dawned in the warden's deep-set eyes. "The homing instinct *is* a strong one, isn't it?"

"Officer Crane?" The dark-haired young man smiled and held out a friendly hand. "I'm Roger Norris. I called this morning."

The blocky policeman rose from his desk, grasping the hand firmly. "Oh, yes. I was told you'd be coming." He looked at Norris' companion, another tall lad who looked more like a country boy, in spite of his sharp suit.

"This is my collaborator, Bob Macklin." Norris indicated the other man. "We represent *Black Book Detective* magazine."

"How d'you do?" Crane stood awkwardly, not sure whether to offer his hand to the other man. Macklin just smiled shyly. "Well, let's all sit down, shall we?"

Once they were seated, Crane focussed his attention on Norris, who had already shown himself to be the more gregarious of the two. "Welcome to Drumright, gentlemen. The chief tells me you want to interview somebody about this station."

"Yes, that's right." Norris drew a notepad from an inside pocket and began writing in it with a pencil stub. "As the man in charge of the station at night, I'm sure you've run into a great deal of criminal activity."

The policeman shrugged modestly, but said nothing.

Norris went on. "Anyway, we at *Black Book* have noticed a significant upsurge in the number of bank holdups recently, particularly in this area. I understand a bank robber and murderer escaped from McAlester Penitentiary just two days ago." He paused and looked up from his pad.

"You mean Virgil Ballard. Yes, I have a flier on him here somewhere." He began shuffling through the untidy stacks of paper on his desk.

Norris held up a hand. "That won't be necessary,"

he said. "We received one yesterday. The article Mr. Macklin and I are preparing will deal with the precautions that small constabularies such as your own are taking to apprehend fugitives such as Ballard."

Crane smiled confidently. "We're quite capable of handling that scum here in Drumright."

Macklin, the country boy, stiffened in his seat. "Yeah," he snapped. "I'll bet you're good at handling scum."

The officer winced at the unexpected retort, and was about to say something equally savage, when Roger Norris spoke in a soothing voice. "Don't pay any attention to my colleague, Officer Crane. I'm afraid he's one of those people who are fascinated by gangsters." He turned to Macklin. "Bob, be quiet and let the officer talk."

The other man seethed, but he didn't say anything.

"Now," said Norris, flipping to a fresh page in the notepad, "about the crime-fighting techniques in Drumright."

"I think you'll find that this station is as well-equipped to deal with your average holdup man as any. Better than most, in fact." The policeman was still rankled by Macklin's outburst, but his confidence was returning.

Norris stopped writing and looked up. "Some of the bigger stations have machine guns."

The officer nodded proudly. "We have machine guns. Bullet-proof vests, too."

The reporters looked at each other. "Really?" said Norris, eyebrows raised. "Could we see them?"

"Sure. They're in the locker. Come on." Crane got up and led the way to the rear of the station house, where a massive gun locker towered in the corner. He unlocked it with a key attached to his belt and swung open the door.

Norris whistled. A row of six brand-new Thompson submachine guns gleamed in the diffused light from the ceiling, their carved wooden grips cocked at an upward angle. On the shelf below them, arranged in an overlapping pattern, was an equal number of hefty-looking quilted vests which resembled the chest protectors worn by baseball catchers. Boxes of ammunition were stacked neatly in the bottom of the lockers, as were extra steel drums for the machine guns.

Norris didn't take his eyes from the guns as he asked, "Mind if I look at one?"

Crane smiled and lifted out one of the weapons, handing it carefully to the reporter. Norris stroked it and slid back the breech quite expertly.

"I see you know how to handle a rifle," commented the officer.

"I've done some shooting, mostly on target ranges." Norris let the action slam shut with a satisfying crack. He looked up. "Is it loaded now?"

"Yes, it is; be careful."

"I will." The reporter hugged the machine gun to his waist and swung the barrel into Crane's midsection. "Stick 'em up."

The other man, Macklin, heaved a second gun from the locker, racked in a shell, and pointed it at the officer.

Crane hadn't yet grasped what was happening. "Be careful with those," he admonished. "They're loaded."

Macklin sneered. "Shut up and reach!"

Now the officer understood what was happening. His eyes swept the station hopefully, searching for another blue uniform like his own. There was none. Meekly, he raised his hands. "Who are you?"

"None of your business." It was Macklin who had spoken. His face was hard and his voice had taken on a new authority. Balancing the Thompson on one forearm, he reached into the locker and hefted out another, which he tossed to his companion, and tucked yet another machine gun under his free arm. "Let's go." He backed toward the door, keeping both weapons trained on the astonished officer.

Norris, equally armed, and with three extra drums of ammunition clapped beneath his right arm, hesitated. "What about the vests?"

"Fuck the vests," shot the other. "Jesus Christ, we don't want no goddamn vests!" He began moving faster.

The other man backed out more slowly. Crane stared at the muzzles of the two machine guns as they moved away. Then the door slammed shut.

Outside the station, Alex Kern turned and picked up speed, trotting toward the white Buick coupe parked beside the curb. "Okay, let's take off."

"Just a second." Virgil Ballard leaned one of his machine guns against the nearby "No Parking" sign and wheeled to face the police station. He crouched and squeezed the other gun tighter against his hip.

Alex's eyes grew wide. "Virge! No!"

Virgil aimed the Thompson at the big front window and cut loose. Yellow flame stuttered from the barrel. The glass shivered and fell apart, sending a hail of glittering slivers onto the sidewalk. The black letters that spelled out "Drumright Police" separated and collapsed, the metal frame that held them wrenched free, and the whole mess caved inward, disappearing beneath the bottom edge of the window.

Inside the station, Officer Crane hit the floor just as a huge shard of glass knifed through the air where his head had been and shattered against the bare brick wall. He resolved to remain where he was until the commotion was over.

The pattern of bullets tripped up the outside wall, exploded a globe light above the front door, and ripped across the metal plaque marked "Police." Then the gun jammed. Virgil was struggling with it when Alex punched the Buick's starter and brought the engine into action with a roar. Virgil gave up and climbed into the car. He leaned out and snatched the extra machine gun from the "No Parking" sign just as the wheels grabbed and began rolling.

Chapter Ten

Chester Hollis bounced and swayed with the gyrations of the old truck as it roared over the top of the hill and descended toward Picher. Seated as he was with his legs dangling off the back of the trailer, he contemplated the Oklahoma landscape as it receded rapidly before his eyes and wondered how much of it was going to be taken over by the banks by the end of the month. It was likely that his fellow oil workers in the box were thinking the same thing, because they, too, were silent for the most part, perhaps only half listening to Luke Shiver's harmonica as it trilled over "Red River Valley" near the front of the truck.

Chester himself had little to fear from the banks' proposed foreclosures, since he and his wife Flora had paid off the mortgage on their half acre on the other side of Picher over a year before, but many of his friends were not so fortunate. His best friends, the ones with whom he had gone to school so many years before, owned farmland that was mortgaged to the hilt on the edges of the vast oil fields. This was the property that would be snatched up by the panic-stricken banks, these the people who would be forced to lead a drifting, nomadic existence once their roots had been destroyed. It was enough to make him throw up his hands in despair, yet it was also enough to make him feel grateful, for the first time in his life, for the dirty, rigorous, but relatively secure position he held working for the oil company.

Luke must have noticed the melancholy that had settled over the tired group, for his harmonica stopped in the middle of a refrain and launched itself immediately into the livelier strains of "Ma, He's Making Eyes at Me." The mood of the others began to perk up, and some of them joined in singing.

Chester formed the words in his head, but he didn't sing along. He was thinking about his friends. He watched the reddening sun as it descended over the distant mountain range, eyeing the shrinking space between them. It didn't look like it was planning to come up again.

The truck bounced to a sudden stop, almost tossing Chester and a few others off the back. He twisted and craned his neck so that he could see above the peeling wooden sideboards. They had stopped before the entrance to Picher's main street. Chester could see the blacktop just beyond the truck's discolored windshield, while the road behind the trailer was unpaved gravel. Something red glared and pulsated in the mouth of the wide street. "Cops," commented a blackened worker at Chester's shoulder. "Don't tell me old Snail-ass is gettin' a ticket for speedin'!"

A state trooper appeared around the end of the trailer, wearing a buff-colored uniform and campaign hat. His right hand rested on the butt of his holstered gun. He stared into the oil workers' faces one by one. "You fellers got names?"

Chester led off with his full name, followed by the others. Luke Shivers took his harmonica out of his mouth just long enough to give his name to the trooper, then thrust it back against his lips and began a subdued version of "Yes, Sir, That's My Baby."

The officer turned to the paunchy truck driver, who had just joined him. "That right?"

"Yes, sir, officer," nodded the driver. "I've known most of these men all my life. They're all good old boys."

"All right, then," said the other. "You can take 'er on through. But don't stop. For nothing. These boys mean business." He gave the trailer a smart slap, like a horse, and disappeared behind the sideboard. The driver followed him.

While the other workers engaged in speculation among themselves over what was transpiring, Chester strained his ears to hear what the driver and the policeman were saying. The driver swore once, good-naturedly, and the other said something that sounded like "Ballard," but that was all Chester could hear. The name meant nothing to him.

The engine growled, turned over, and the truck jolted into motion, passing the stationary police car as its master stood beside it with one foot propped up on the dusty running board. There was another marked car on the opposite side of the street, and Chester noticed a group of uniformed men standing in the doorway of the Picher Print shop, their shadows stretching to the middle of the street in the late afternoon sun. Something was about to happen. He couldn't help but wonder what it was.

As the truck rumbled past the cafe, Chester made up his mind. He snatched up his black lunch pail and hopped off the end of the trailer.

"Hey, Chester!" hollered one of the oil workers from inside the box. "Where you goin'?"

Chester cupped his hands around his mouth and yelled back: "Get me a bite to eat! You guys go on!" He waved and stepped into the little cafe.

The skinny cook looked up from the counter and smiled as Chester entered, her buck teeth showing over her lower lip. "Hi, there, Mr. Hollis," she said. "Ain't seen you since God knows when."

Chester smiled back. "Cuppa coffee, Amy, please," he said, and took a stool that afforded him a good view through the window.

Hazel had seen the state trooper before he came through the door of the print shop downstairs. He had paused by his car as the big truck pulled away, then turned and pushed his way through the other three officers positioned in the doorway of the brick building in which she kept her apartment.

Hazel's heart began thumping. At first she didn't know what to do. She thought of leaving, but there was only one way to get to the ground floor, and that led down the very staircase that the officer would soon be using to get to her room. Then she remembered Virgil's letter.

Swiftly, because she fancied she heard the trooper's heavy tread on the staircase, Hazel punched open the overlapping panels that were used to adjust the volume on the Victrola, drew out the letter that Virgil had sent her from Drumright, and set fire to it with the aid of a kitchen match. The flame took hold and bloomed a bright yellow, hungrily devouring the thin paper. She dropped the flaming fragment into an empty glass on the pantry table just as she heard a board creak outside her door, then slapped it out with her hand and wafted the dry smoke through the open window. Then she answered the door.

The trooper was so big he filled the tall doorway. He was holding his campaign hat in his hands. Hazel felt herself growing faint, and forced a smile. "Yes?"

"State police, miss," answered the trooper in an official-sounding baritone. "I'm Sergeant Fowler."

"Is there something I can do for you, Sergeant?"

Fowler's eyes were hard. "Yes, ma'am. You can stay right here."

Hazel put on a surprised expression. "Whatever for? Is there something wrong?"

"There won't be, if you do what I say." He stepped into the room without waiting for an invitation. His well-cropped hair almost touched the ceiling, and Hazel was reminded of the difference between Virgil's height and Fowler's. And Virgil was far from short.

He stood just inside the doorway, looking around. Hazel caught her breath when his eyes lighted on the glass, but they moved on again, sweeping the rest of the apartment. "What's in there?" he demanded, indicating the door on the opposite wall.

"Just the bedroom," she replied, and injected a seductive note into her voice. "Would you like me to show it to you?"

"No." The sergeant actually blushed and turned away from the door.

"Look, Sergeant, would you tell me what this is all about?" She was becoming angry.

Fowler looked at her smugly. "Quit the playacting, lady. You know as well as me that your boyfriend's coming to see you. Maybe tonight.

"What boyfriend?"

"Ballard. Virgil Ballard, as if you didn't know. Your boyfriend. The one who sent you the letter you just burned —" he nodded toward the glass with the curl of carbon in the bottom — "and put out with this hand." He took her right hand and turned it over, revealing the black smudge on the bottom of her palm.

Hazel snatched her hand away. "You've got it all figured out, haven't you, Sergeant?" There was a knife edge in her voice.

"We try. I'm sending an officer up to stay here with you until we have Ballard in custody — or dead. I wouldn't worry about him; unlike your boyfriend, Officer Gordon is a perfect gentleman." He put on his hat and opened the door, then gazed down at her. "Behave yourself." Then he left.

Hazel waited, steaming, until the big sergeant's footsteps retreated down the stairs. Then she grabbed her purse from the table and headed for the door.

A blocky-looking policeman was standing in front of the door. He touched his hat brim. "Officer Gordon, ma'am," he said. "I'll be out here if you need me."

Hazel slammed the door so hard it disappeared behind the jamb.

The hood of the little coupe glowed red in the rays of the departing sun as Virgil braked to a stop in front of the Picher Print Shop. He climbed out and looked up at Hazel's bedroom window, but the fierce glare from the west made a completely opaque surface of the single pane.

The street was deserted. It was that time of day when the worktime activity of the small town had ground to a stop and everyone was taking a breather before launching into their nocturnal pastimes at the cafe and the tiny speakeasy at the other end of the town. For this reason, Virgil felt no suspicion when nobody appeared on the sidewalk. He did, however, feel lonely, and almost wished that Alex Kern had joined him instead of remaining in Commerce. Almost, but not quite. It had been hard enough to talk Alex into laying over an extra night before heading across the state line without having him drive. Of the two, Virgil was the only real driver.

He stepped up onto the sidewalk, shot one glance back at the car to reassure himself that the trunk lid was locked securely over the single machine gun he had brought with him, and turned toward the print shop. He was just about to push open the door when he noticed something strange.

It took him a few seconds to realize what it was,

and when he did, he began backing carefully across the sidewalk toward his car. The presses weren't running. Virgil knew the old printer who ran the shop, knew him well enough to know that he never let his presses cool off until well after sundown. But the silence that had greeted him at the door was enough to warn him that something had interfered with the printer's schedule, and that something could only be one thing. With this in mind, he backed off the curb and drew his new Luger from its holster beneath his jacket.

"Freeze!" shouted a voice from behind him.

Virgil whirled to face a local policeman standing in the middle of the street, his revolver steadied in two outstretched hands. Virgil fired from the hip. His bullet struck the officer's cap with a sharp slap and sent it spinning off his head.

The cop, surprised, hesitated for an instant before returning the fire. It was all Virgil needed. He hit the street and rolled just as the bullet passed through the spot where he had been standing, and came up on the driver's side of the car. He snapped off a wild shot that nevertheless sent the policeman ducking for cover on the opposite side of the street. Then something smacked the side of the coupe, and Virgil turned to see a uniformed state trooper in the doorway of the print shop, a curl of smoke spiraling up from the barrel of his pistol. The fugitive fired point-blank at him and missed.

Now men in uniform came pouring out all over the street. They appeared in the alleys, came out of the buildings, and rose from behind low board fences alongside the sidewalks, each bearing a weapon. Some had shotguns, and Virgil saw the sun glint on their barrels as they were brought into play. Lead screamed from every direction, skinning within inches of Virgil's head and plowing deep into the wooden frame buildings that lined the street. It had suddenly become very difficult to survive in Picher, Oklahoma, if one's name was Virgil Ballard.

Chester Hollis was cemented to his stool in the cafe up the street, watching the spectacle open-mouthed. The skinny cook had fled screaming out the back door after the first shot. On the range behind the counter, Hollis' coffee, unattended, boiled over and sizzled on the hot griddle. He paid it no heed.

The snapping and popping and zinging that came to his ears from the other side of the big plate glass window was something new in his experience, as was the sight of armed men darting back and forth and firing at each other. It was like a movie, only real, larger than life, and being played for his benefit alone. He wouldn't have missed it for all the oil in Oklahoma.

The object of it all, the man crouching beside the bullet-spattered automobile, suddenly rose and fired at some unseen danger to his left. Hollis slid off the stool to see what it was. At that instant, the plate glass window bloomed at head level, collapsing in a shower of flashing pieces. He never heard them hit the floor. The bullet struck him in the forehead and he sat back down, dead.

Virgil laid down a pattern of gunfire in a half circle around him and leaped behind the wheel of the coupe. A bullet smashed through the windshield and whizzed past the brim of his hat as he hit the starter. The engine exploded into operation, the tires squealed, and the car careened down the middle of the street, its driver hunched low behind the dashboard.

Then the second part of the trap sprang shut. Without warning, a black and white patrol car pulled out of a side street and stopped, blocking the north end of the main thoroughfare. Virgil hit the brakes and tore the wheel to the left. The white coupe screamed into a 180-degree turn, its rear end skidding around within inches of striking a lamppost on the right. Then it leaped forward again, hurtling southward.

Another patrol car came out to block that exit, and thus drive home the last part of the trap. Virgil saw its nose come sliding out of the alley and stomped down on the accelerator. The engine howled. A blast of wind whipped his hat off and bounced it into the back seat. Through the windshield he saw the body of the police car join the nose, could make out the features of the officer in the driver's seat as he turned to watch the coupe slow down.

But Virgil didn't slow down. The foot pedal was against the floorboards now, and the roar in his ears had cut out every other sound. The scenery sped past him, a shapeless blur. He grimaced and slumped down in his seat in preparation for the impact that was coming.

The driver of the patrol car stared, his mouth working soundlessly. He stopped the car two thirds of the way across the street and disappeared beneath the bottom of the window. The coupe's engine became a whine. Then they collided.

Metal screamed against metal in a grotesque parody of human anguish. The torpedo-shaped prow of the Buick coupe hooked the patrol car's left front fender, lifted it, and sent the front end of the black-and-white arcing into a fire hydrant near the curb. From it erupted a gray-white geyser of shimmering water, the drops of which screened the mangled escape vehicle's movements as it left Picher behind a shower of mud.

From her vantage point at the window, Hazel watched Virgil as he came backing around the front of his car, firing his Luger about him. She had wanted to throw open the window, to lean out and see everything that was happening, but Officer Gordon's firm grip on her arm had held her back. He had joined her a moment after the white Buick had been sighted, and it had been his thick hand across her mouth that had stopped her from calling out when Virgil stepped onto the sidewalk. Now she was forced to sit and watch in silence, knowing that there was nothing she could do to help.

Moments after the collision and subsequent escape of the fugitive vehicle, the door in the apartment opened and Sergeant Fowler came in, removing his hat before it was crushed against the ceiling. His face was strangely calm.

"How the hell did he get away?" asked Officer Gordon incredulously, then remembered Hazel and blushed. "Sorry, miss."

Fowler was unmoved. "We'd of got him right off

the bat if we didn't have to rely on the locals. But he won't get far."

"What makes you say that?" Hazel challenged.

"Because very few people escape an all-points bulletin on foot. One of those bullets drove right through his gas tank." He stood looking at her for a long moment, then beckoned to Gordon, and the two went out, leaving Hazel alone with her thoughts.

Part III

Tri-State Terror

It is getting light in the east, but it will be a long time before the sun comes up to challenge the black ceiling of the clouds. The rain is coming harder now, pelting the puddles and washing down the steep hill which the lawmen are climbing. It forms eddies in the gutter, pounds on the empty oil drums beside the nearby service station, and begins to wash away the brown stains on the pavement.

Special agent William Farnum holds his machine gun with the muzzle pointed downward, so that the water will not enter the barrel. The flashlights of his men dart back and forth like fireflies on both sides of the street, probing and searching the darkened garages, sweeping the empty lots and back alleys. No response.

Up ahead, the single unarmed agent is having trouble keeping the hounds' leashes from tangling. They have calmed down to some degree, and are wandering around, crossing and recrossing each other's path in search of a scent, their noses loudly snuffling the wet pavement. Their wet coats glisten in the pale beam of Farnum's light.

None of this makes any impression on the chief of the government men, for his mind is elsewhere. His ears are attuned to every sound outside of those his fellow officials are making, his eyes constantly roving in search of any unexplained movement. Six months ago, four special agents in Kansas City lost their lives while escorting a prisoner to jail because they weren't paying attention to what was going on around them. Nothing like that is going to happen here, if Farnum can help it. He rubs his eyes occasionally, to clear them of raindrops. He is cold; but so, he knows, is his prey.

From here, the street climbs steadily upward, heading toward the rolling prairie ridges on the horizon. Houses, shops, and offices face each other across the wide street. Any one of them could be a refuge for the one they seek, but the bloodstains continue up the street.

A front door is flung open with a bang on Farnum's right. He wheels, clapping his Thompson to his hip. A hand appears across a lighted threshhold and a large brown cat is deposited onto the porch. It shakes itself, stretches the length of its legs, and, as the door is slammed shut once again, ambles down the wooden steps onto the street. The lawmen chuckle, the tension relaxes for a moment. Then they resume the hunt.

Chapter Eleven

August 1, 1931.

"Snap off. It's time to go back." The fat guard was a black shape against the setting sun.

Virgil stretched mightily and went over to throw his shovel into the back of the truck along with those of his fellow prisoners. Then the half-ton Model T started up and took off, leaving the guards and the convicts to make their way back to McAlester on foot.

Slowly, because they were tired, the gray-clad men formed a single line and, prodded by the rifle-toting guards, began marching down the narrow dirt road. In the lush treetops far above their heads, two unseen birds whistled a mournful goodnight to each other that must have pared the convicts hearts to the core. Everything else was so damned free. But the road stretched onward relentlessly, unheeding in its inevitable progress toward the world that existed behind stone walls.

After they had gone abut a quarter of a mile, Virgil saw his chance. The guard up front and the one in the rear turned their attention away from the phalanx of prisoners to watch a grizzled farmer wrestle with an overturned tractor in a nearby field. Without a sound, Virgil slipped out of line then ducked behind a tangle of bushes. Then the others closed ranks, quietly and efficiently.

Virgil crouched in the bush for long seconds, the thorny twigs pricking his skin. While he waited, the sun slipped beneath the horizon, bathing the scene in a lavender glow and etching the bobbing forms in a silhouette of dark purple. The last man in line had nearly passed before his eyes when the guard in the rear noticed the absence. "Hey!" he shouted to the man up front. "We got a con missing!"

The fugitive took advantage of the confusion and bolted from the bush, heading downhill toward the bluff of the river that wound parallel to the road. He leaped into the water, just as something zinged past him and plucked at his shirt sleeve. It was followed almost immediately by a sharp crack from behind him.

Virgil hit the water and began swimming. His hands and feet churned and crashed through the cold water, supplementing and at times surpassing the swift current that carried him farther and farther away with each beat of his heart, doubling and redoubling the distance between him and his pursuers. Bullets chopped and splashed all around him, a few even sang within an inch of his right ear, but he was too busy scooping a progress through the dense river to take much notice. He ducked beneath the surface at frequent intervals to avoid as much fire as possible. At last, nearly a mile from the spot where he had dived in, Virgil crawled out, panting but unscathed, onto the opposite bank of the river. He lay there a moment to catch his breath, then scrambled to his feet and charged off into the scrub oak. It was almost dark.

Alex Kern looked the picture of prosperity as he led the way through the glass doors of the Wichita Savings and Loan Company. He was wearing a dark black suit of some shiny material with matching vest and set off by a bright red tie, the initials of which, elegantly woven into the silky material just beneath the knot, were not his own. The fawn-colored spats he had buttoned snugly over his gleaming black shoes were carefully chosen, for they matched exactly the expensive snap-brim hat he wore tilted over his right eye. He carried his small suitcase so effortlessly that no one would have guessed the heavy object it contained.

Virgil, entering on his heels, cut a similar but more subdued figure in a modest suit and darker felt hat, and carrying a suitcase identical to his partner's. Together, they crossed the highly waxed floor past the tellers' cages, set their burdens on the elbow-high bench along the far wall, and opened them. It was the work of a few seconds to assemble the lethal weapons and attach the drum clips. They were so efficient about it, in fact, that none of the bank's customers knew what was happening until the two strangers racked the first shells into the barrels and moved away from the bench. Then the small crowd fanned out in every direction, eyes on the two machine guns, hands in the air.

Alex smiled with all his teeth. "That's it, folks," he said, balancing his weapon on one forearm, "just stay back and keep your hand away from your sides. . . . And stay away from the door!" He swung the gun on a middle-aged guard who had been inching toward the entrance. The guard stopped and moved away obediently.

"Down on the floor!" snapped Virgil, striding to the middle of the room. He held his machine gun tightly in both hands. "Now!"

The patrons reacted quickly to this prompting, and prostrated themselves, faces down, on the tile floor. "Not you," said Virgil, glancing at the bank employees standing behind the long counter, some of whom had been in the act of lowering themselves to the raised platform in back of the cages. A fat man in a suit of some English cut was having trouble lowering his huge frame until Virgil placed the barrel of his weapon underneath the man's nose. Then he hit the floor like a felled oak.

Kern took a black cloth sack from his open suitcase, shook it free of its folds, and went over to the nearest cage, where he shoved it in front of a diminutive female teller. Her heavily mascaraed eyes widened visibly.

"Well?" he said calmly.

"Well . . . what?" The girl's voice was barely audible.

Alex's sunny manner vanished. "Fill it. To the top."

The teller hesitated a moment, then took the bag

and began stuffing stacks of bills into it from her cash drawer.

While she was busy with this, Virgil came forward and stepped around the end of the varnished counter. "Which one of you is in charge?" His eyes swept the line of bank employees standing against the back wall, hands raised.

A small man near the end stirred. "I'm the chief cashier," he volunteered.

Virgil looked at him. The little teller looked quaint and birdlike with his pinch-nose glasses perched atop his shining beak. The green eye-shade and striped sleeve garters he wore added to the illusion, making him look like some rare species of prairie chicken. He didn't appear to be frightened, though his face was pale. "You know the combination to the vault?" Virgil waved the barrel of his gun toward the circular steel door looming massively on the wall behind the wooden cages.

After a minute, the man nodded. "I do."

"Open it."

"No."

Virgil raised his eyebrows and glanced at Alex on the other side of the counter. His partner was smiling incredulously, gold tooth shining. Virgil turned back to the cashier and poked the muzzle of his Thompson into the man's face. "Open it," he repeated.

The cashier shook his head and paled a shade further. The bank robber snatched the little man by his collar and drew him close, shoving the gun beneath his chin. The man grunted. "I'll blow your goddamn head off!" Virgil's voice was rising.

"I'm not allowed to open the vault unless the president is here." Sweat broke out on the teller's face, but his tone was emphatic.

Virgil signaled to his partner. Alex knew what to do. He reached between the bars of the teller's cage, grabbed the female employee roughly by the shoulder, and thrust his machine gun against her neck at an upward angle. She whimpered, but didn't move.

"Now," whispered Virgil to the head teller, "if you don't open the vault, this pretty little girl's brains will be splattered all over your nice clean bank. You want that?"

The cashier began to shake uncontrollably. Virgil yanked him off his feet. "Answer me!"

"I —" he gasped. "I can't. The rules —"

"Shoot her!"

There was a long silence. Virgil shot a glance at Alex. "What are you waiting for? Shoot her!"

Alex looked as pale as the girl he was holding. "I can't, Virge! Not just like that! Not in cold blood."

"You weak-kneed son of a bitch!" Virgil released the chief cashier and swung the barrel of his machine gun so that it pointed at the girl's mid-section. She squirmed in Alex Kern's frightened grip and cried out hoarsely. Virgil had flipped the gun onto single shot and was about to squeeze the trigger when the chief cashier interrupted him.

"Wait!" he screamed. "I'll open the vault."

"Boy, oh, boy!" Virgil rammed the shift lever into third and the heavy Oldsmobile left the ground, bouncing along the gravel road. "I never thought I'd be teaming up with a goddamn humanitarian! Boy, oh, boy!"

Alex held on tight to the dashboard. "I'm sorry Virge. I told you before I wasn't no murderer."

They rode in silence for a long time, watching the rutted cow path disappear beneath the sedan's hungry wheels. Finally Virgil spoke. "How much we get?"

"Lemme see." Alex hefted the black cloth bag from the floor to the seat beside him. He began counting in stacks of a thousand. "Six, seven, eight, nine. . . ."

Virgil thought back to the days of Roy Farrell and the Moss boys. They had only gotten eight thousand in Apache. He wondered what those boys were doing now.

". . . Twenty, twenty-one, twenty-two. . . ."

The Kansas countryside shot past the window, flat as a table top. There was a lot more green in the scenery than there was in Oklahoma. And a lot more green, Virgil mused, in the banks.

". . . Fifty-three. . . . These others is in five-hundred-dollar stacks. . . . Fifty-four, five, six. . . ." He turned to Virgil, astonished. "Jesus Christ, we topped sixty grand!"

Virgil smiled and swerved around a particularly vicious-looking pothole. "The vault, boy. That's where the money is." He shook his head. "To think that little sonuvabitch cashier almost kept us from getting into it. And you damn near helped him do it!"

"Cut it out. We got into it, didn't we? We didn't have to kill nobody to do it, either."

"Stupid bastard." Virgil spoke as if he hadn't heard Kern's remark. "I almost wish he'd give me an excuse to cut him down."

He felt Alex watching him, and turned to face his partner. "What are you gaping at?" he demanded.

Alex shifted his eyes to the road ahead. "Nothing."

"What do you mean, nothing? You was looking at me like you just found out I laid your old lady or something. What's wrong?"

The other shrugged and avoided his eyes. "Nothing. Just thinking."

They drove on in silence.

Earl Bishop swung shut the door of his patrol car and looked up at the stone facade that loomed above him. It was a hotel building, one of the newer ones in Wichita, its edges as clean and as sharp as new cardboard. Young though he was, in his fresh blue uniform and highly polished black visor, Patrolman Bishop seemed to go with these surroundings. He entered through the revolving door.

Once inside, he spotted the desk clerk, an alert-looking young man about his own age, and went over to him. "You in charge?" Bishop asked.

"I am until Mr. Wattler gets back from lunch. He's the manager." The young clerk looked concerned. "Is something wrong?"

Bishop took a square of paper from the pocket of his tunic, unfolded it, and handed it to the clerk. "Is this man staying in your hotel?"

The clerk studied the circular. In the center, beneath the alarming black "Wanted," was the picture of a pleasant-looking young man with fine features and a thick shock of black hair. He was smiling. "I'm not sure," said the clerk slowly. "I haven't been here too long."

"How about him?" The policeman handed him a similar document. A morose blond fellow with a pouting look stared coldly from the center of this one. The clerk recognized him instantly. "Sure!" he exclaimed. "He registered about a week ago." He flipped through the pages of the open book at his elbow. "Here! This is it!" He turned the book so that the officer could read the hastily scrawled signature beneath his finger: "Oscar Miller, Room 280."

Bishop noted the room number. "Is he in now?"

The clerk turned to look at the key board behind the desk. "He must be. His key's gone. You going up?"

The officer ignored the question. "Is he alone?"

"Search me."

"No need." Bishop headed for the carpeted staircase that would take him to the second floor. He hesitated with one foot on the bottom step and glanced back at the clerk. "There'll be a few more police coming in a little while," he said. "Send 'em on up, will you?"

"Will do."

Room 280 was the second door on the left. The policeman paused in front of it and listened. Music drifted out faintly from inside the room, and once he heard a bedspring creak. He took a deep breath and knocked boldly on the door.

Virgil was stretched out on the bed in his pin-striped trousers and BVD undershirt, smoking a cigarette. Beside him, the big floor model RCA vibrated as Bix Beiderbecke seized "Baby, Won't You Please Come Home?" from the rest of Frankie Trumbauer's orchestra, pushed it through his trumpet, and gave it a whole new dimension. Virgil sang along with it quietly, waving his ash-laden cigarette in time to the jumping music. The knock on the door cut him off in midlyric.

Sitting up abruptly, he put his cigarette out in the ashtray atop the radio. Alex and he had agreed upon a special knock should he come to visit the other, and that wasn't it. He reached beneath his pillow, picked up his Luger, and slipped quietly out of bed.

Earl Bishop had his fist raised to knock again when the door opened. For what seemed an eternity, he stood staring into the hardened face of the man he had come to get. Then the Luger barked. Something tore into his guts, burning a white-hot swath as it passed through him from belly to back. He clutched at his abdomen and felt his intestines squirm in his hands. Hot blood flowed over his fingers. Then he fell.

Virgil stepped over the policeman's body and catapulted through the doorway, straight into the arms of two more men in uniform. Something came down hard on the back of his head and he collapsed, but not before the toe of a glossily polished boot struck him in the groin. The floor came up almost as hard.

Chapter Twelve

BALLARD ESCAPES! screamed the two-inch-high headline. Tri-State Terror With Ten Others in Mass Break! Four columns went on to describe the details of the incident at the Kansas State Prison in Lansing.

Hazel rolled up the newspaper and slid it into the waste basket beside her desk. A colored section advertising a special Memorial Day Sale at Miami's biggest department store slipped free and fell to the floor. She sat there a long time, staring at the colorful debris. Then she snapped out of it and turned back to her typewriter.

Hazel was nearly thirty now, but she didn't look it. Her black hair showed no signs of gray and her oval face was unlined. The colorful print dress she was wearing contributed to the youthful image, as did the lighter make-up she had taken to using. At twenty-nine, Hazel appared to have been in suspended animation for five years. Which was very close to the truth.

She hadn't been with Virgil for over five years, not since that traumatic visit she had paid him soon after he had been incarcerated in McAlester, when he had advised her not to wait for him. Despite his advice, she had not had anything to do with any man since. Not that she hadn't been asked; the office here in Miami was full of back-room lotharios who had been more than willing to "show her a good time" — which meant, of course, the nearest hotel or the back seat of a borrowed touring car. She had turned them all down.

Now, sitting here, typing up a bit of correspondence between her boss and the head of a similar firm in another city, Hazel asked herself for the thousandth time why she hadn't accepted those invitations. And, for the thousandth time, she came up with the same answer: Virgil Ballard. There had never been anyone but Virgil. It had been that way ever since they had first caught sight of each other, so long ago, in the little one-room schoolhouse just outside of Picher. It would always be that way. She loved him now as she lived him then, only stronger, because he had been away. She simply could not see herself going with anybody but Virgil Ballard.

The sad thing about it was that it was probably over. Two years had passed since the shootout in the streets of Picher, two years during which Virgil had had ample time to get over whatever affection he had once felt for her. In that time, he had looted banks, traded bullets with the law, paced the floor of at least two prison cells — and met other women. There was something about the smell of gunpowder, Hazel knew, that could make a man forget his first love. After all, hadn't he given her her freedom back in 1927? Why shouldn't he expect the same?

Mr. Simpson poked his head out his office door. He was a big man, with a ruddy complexion and thinning gray hair. "Are you still here?" He mocked anger. "It's Memorial Day, Hazel. Go home."

"But Mr. Simpson, I have all this work to do. These letters —"

He waved her protests away. "It's late. Go home. Get some sleep. And I better not catch you in this office before noon!"

Hazel smiled, and said, "Thank you," but she said it to a closed door. She stacked the papers neatly, replaced the cover on her typewriter, took her purse and hat from the clothes tree behind her desk, and left.

The night air, one flight down from the office, was cool and comfortable. Hazel stepped briskly through the small employees' parking lot and got into her automobile. It was a Hudson sedan, not exactly a brand-new 1933 model, but large and spacious and dependable. The high front seat creaked when she sat on it.

"What? No chauffeur?"

Hazel jumped, nearly knocking off her hat on the upholstered ceiling. In the rear-view mirror, Virgil's sunny face smiled impishly from the back seat. "Home, James," he said.

"Vir —!" exclaimed Hazel, turning around, but she was cut off when two lips pressed firmly and passionately against her own.

The loudly ticking clock on the bedside table read 2:30. Hazel nuzzled against Vrigil's bare chest and drew the thin sheet up to her neck. She sighed. Sometime during the night, the moonlight had sneaked through the window of the hotel room, and now it illuminated their relaxed bodies.

"Virgil?" she said sweetly.

"Mmmmm?"

She twisted her head to look up at him. "How'd you know where to find me?"

He smiled sleepily. "Love finds a way."

"No, I mean it."

He grunted and rubbed his eyes. "I couldn't very well go back to Picher after what happened last time," he said yawning. "So I took a chance and came here to see if I could find you at work. I got lucky."

"But you didn't know what car I was driving."

"I read the registration of every car in the lot."

"Oh." There was a stretch of silence, broken only by the sound of Virgil's even breathing as he slipped back into sleep. Then, "Virgil?"

His eyes sprang open. "What?"

"What happened in Kansas?"

"Nothing much. Me and ten other guys got sick of rotting while we was still alive. We got guns." He took a cigarette from the pocket of his jacket hanging on the bedpost, lit it. "It wasn't pretty."

"I guess not." Hazel began to relax again, then

remembered something and stiffened. "Did you read what the papers are calling you?"

Virgil snorted. "The Tri-State Terror. That's a laugh." He spat out his cigarette smoke.

"That's not all. The government men say you're Public Enemy Number One."

"Yeah?" He looked thoughtful. "I didn't know that."

"They say you don't last long once they make you Number One."

Virgil didn't answer.

"Marry me, Virgil."

He didn't make a sound for a long time. Then he dragged in a lungful of smoke and let it out slowly though his nostrils. "You're on," he said and crushed her to him.

The youngster looked up at Virgil, an eager light snapping in his clear blue eyes. He was small and slight and wore big horn-rimmed glasses that kept sliding down his freckled ski nose. His hair was so blond it was almost white and was getting thin in front. Virgil appraised him quickly, then looked to Alex Kern for an explanation.

"I been telling you about Boyd Harriman," said Alex, his hand on the youngster's shoulder. "Boyd's hell with a machine gun."

The boy smiled shyly, but didn't say anything.

Virgil regarded him through narrowed eyes. Standing as he was, his frail frame dwarfed against the majestic Missouri landscape that surrounded them, he didn't look like much. "How old are you, kid?"

"Twenty-three." He had a high-pitched voice, squeaky and irritating.

"Hell, this punk isn't nineteen. What the hell are we running here, a goddamn orphanage?" The question was put to Kern.

Undaunted, Alex replied, "Age don't mean nothing in this business, as long as you're good at what you do. This kid's dynamite, I tell you."

"Yeah. We'll see." Virgil strode over to the car, a new 1933 Plymouth six, stolen, reached through the open back window, and hauled out a Thompson submachine gun. This he carried over to where Boyd Harriman was standing and slammed it into the boy's chest. "Show us," Virgil demanded.

It took Harriman a second to get over the shock of the sudden burden, then he smiled and curled his frail hands lovingly around the big curved grips. He dropped the gun to hip level and let his bespectacled gaze sweep the lush landscape that rolled placidly before him. At last he pointed down the hill. "That tree," he said. "Watch."

He set his feet about a shoulder's width apart, fiddled with the gun. Then he let fly. The gun stuttered long and loud, spitting gleaming brass cartridges from the breech. Bullets spattered against the stout apple tree at the foot of the hill, splitting and splintering the rough black bark as they traveled upward toward the crotch, gouging a ragged bone-white pattern up the middle of the trunk. The branches shook and released a torrent of green leaves and shriveled apples to the ground. When he had finished, the twisted tree looked as if it had been struck by lightning. Not one bullet had gone past the trunk.

Virgil took his eyes from the scarred target and looked at the youngster. Harriman was a vague shape in a blue haze of drifting gunsmoke, a litter of brass cylinders at his feet. The echo of the staccato gunfire rumbled away over the hills like distant thunder.

"Where the hell did you learn to shoot like that?" Virgil wanted to know.

Harriman smiled and let the smoking barrel droop. "My pa smuggled a BAR back from France in '18. Taught me how to use it.

"Boyd was with the Detroit Purple Gang for a year," volunteered Alex. "You learn with those boys."

"Well Mr. Ballard? Do I get the job?" The boy grinned and pushed his eyeglasses back up his nose with his free hand.

"Call me Virgil," said the other, extending his hand.

The next day, Virgil left the office of the Justice of the Peace with his new bride. He was decked out in a light tan suit and spats, and sported a flat straw boater at a rakish angle over his left eye. Hazel had on a tight yellow dress with a bit of lace at the neck. For virginity's sake, a white veil fluttered from her flowered hat. They made an attractive couple as they climbed into the Plymouth six, the "Just Married" sign on the back courtesy Alex Kern and Boyd Harriman, and drove off.

Alex and Boyd met them as they pulled into the driveway of the frame house outside of Stockton, Missouri.

The Stockton Farmer's Bank & Trust job was their smoothest to date. They left the engine running and

Virgil and Boyd, each toting a machine gun, ran through the bank's open door while Alex Kern remained on the sidewalk with a revolver concealed in his jacket pocket. The vault was open behind the marble counter. Boyd stood in the middle of the floor, machine gun leveled at three bank employees and the handful of customers who huddled as far away from the gun as they could get, and Virgil went into the vault and scooped the money into his bag from the file drawers along the concrete walls. When he had finished, he and Boyd hustled back out the door, collected Alex Kern, and were off before the alarm began clanging. It was the best wedding present Virgil could have hoped for.

Chapter Thirteen

It was dusk when the big Plymouth jostled into the driveway of the rented house and braked to a bouncing halt. Hazel, who had been sitting on the couch, reading, put down her copy of *Liberty* and got up to flick on the porch light. She was wearing slippers and a long quilted dressing gown.

Alex Kern and Boyd Harriman piled out of the car and started for the porch. Boyd had his machine gun tucked securely beneath his arm. Alex carried the money bag. Behind them, the car rolled forward toward the garage, Virgil at the wheel.

"What happened?" Hazel asked anxiously when the two had entered.

The black sack thumped heavily onto the linen-covered dining room table, propelled by Alex's long arm. "Only twenty-five thousand dollars, that's all." His face was split by a huge grin.

"Smoothest piece of work I ever saw," piped Boyd. He began breaking down his machine gun and laying the parts on the tablecloth. "Like a clock. The boys in Detroit would of admired it."

Hazel ignored the compliment to her new husband's skill. "Did anybody get hurt?"

"Only the bankers' pocketbooks." Virgil, who had entered through the side door of the garage, came in from the kitchen. He grabbed Hazel, spun her into his arms, and kissed her, hard. She didn't respond. He drew away and studied her in a puzzled way.

"Twenty-five grand, three ways." Alex thought for a moment. "That's over eight thousand apiece."

"Four ways," Virgil corrected him, turning away from Hazel. "We agreed, remember? One cut goes to Hazel because she's in with us."

"Yeah. I forgot."

"That's fair. She gives us respectability when we rent a place to stay." Boyd busied himself with cleaning the machine gun. He blew down the barrel and looked through it at Virgil.

Virgil carried his machine gun, which he had been holding in one hand, over to the narrow closet door and swung it open. Shotguns and pistols and machine guns and open boxes of ammunition gleamed from the closet's interior.

Boyd whistled. "Some arsenal."

"Mostly rented," said Alex, loosening his tie. "Virgil knows a guy in Oklahoma City."

Virgil clapped his machine gun into the closet beside the others and pushed the door shut. "Renting guns is a pain. We got to get some of our own."

Alex said, "How do you plan to do that?"

"Same way as last time."

"Police station?"

Virgil nodded. "There's a place here in Missouri that's perfect. Guns till hell won't have 'em."

"Man!" exclaimed Boyd, impressed. "Rob a police station! You guys got nerve."

Hazel went into the bedroom and slammed the door with a bang.

Alex stared after her. "What's eating her?"

Virgil didn't answer. He went to the bedroom door and gave the knob a yank. It didn't budge. "Hey!" He rattled the knob. "Unlock it, Hazel. Or I'll shoot it off."

"Leave her alone, Virge," said Alex. "You know women. Maybe she just wants to be alone."

"Well, she's not gonna be. Not on our goddamn honeymoon, she isn't." He banged on the door.

After a moment, there was a click. Virgil opened the door and went in, closing it behind him.

Boyd looked at Alex, mirth showing through his big glasses. Alex glared back and began snickering. Then they both laughed out loud.

After unlocking the door, Hazel had gone back to the bed, and now she lay on her back, staring at the bright yellow-papered ceiling. Virgil came in quietly and stood looking down at her. "All right," he sighed, "What is it this time? Sore because I left you alone on our honeymoon."

She didn't answer, but intensified her study of the ceiling.

"Is it because two strange men are coming along on our wedding trip?"

Silence.

"You might as well tell me. I'm going to find out sooner or later."

There was still no response.

Virgil sat down on the edge of the bed. "Why don't you want me to rob banks?"

Hazel stirred. Her gaze swung to her husband for the first time since he had entered the room. "It's not just the banks," she said. "It's everything. You've escaped from three prisons. You're wanted for the murders of three men, one of them a policeman, to say nothing of all the places you've robbed. J. Edgar Hoover made you Public Enemy Number One. The order is out to shoot you on sight." She turned over on her side and looked him full in the face. "Virgil, isn't that enough?" Her pretty features were distorted with mixed anger and anguish.

"So now it comes out." Virgil looked more saddened than annoyed.

"I couldn't hold it back any longer. Give it up, Virgil. There's nothing in it for you anymore."

"Would you rather I turned myself in to the law?" His face darkened. "It'll be the chair, you know. No doubt about it."

"It doesn't have to be that way. There are other countries. Mexico's one. Canada's another. Or South America."

"I'm dead either way."

Silence reigned. A late summer breeze wafted through the window screen and rustled the curtains. Then Virgil spoke again. "Money smells better when it's stolen." His voice was subdued. "It's cleaner than honest money, and crisper and cooler. I like the feel of it. If you ask me why I rob banks, that's the only reason I can give you. I don't have no others."

He stopped talking and glanced at his wife to see if she were going to say anything; she wasn't. He continued. "It's been that way with me since I was in the hills, when I was twenty. I couldn't give that up for any place in South America. It isn't worth it." He tore his eyes from whatever they had been scrutinizing, and turned them back to Hazel. "You can't understand that, can you?"

She studied his face in silence, and suddenly hers brightened. "No, I can't," she said, and threw her arms around him.

Alex was watching when the light coming beneath the bedroom door was snapped off. He smiled slyly at Boyd, who was busy putting his machine gun back together. "Well," he said, stretching, "whatcha wanna do tonight, Boyd?"

"Kansas City?" Alex was befuddled.

Virgil nodded, scratching a faint circle with his fingernail around the black legend on the Missouri road map. "We're gonna hit the First National smack in the middle of the afternoon, right off Main Street. They'll never know what hit 'em." He struck Kansas City with the heel of his hand. Petals came loose from Hazel's marsh marigolds standing in the green cut-glass vase and floated to the table.

"Won't that be breaking your own rule? About hitting the big cities?" Boyd's voice was squeaky but steady.

"That rule's out of style. I made it up when these hick burgs still had money in their banks. Nowadays, every third place we come to is boarded up. It's the cities that pay off these days, and pay off big. Things went pretty smooth in Wichita. Right, Alex?"

Alex made a face. "If you don't count the chief cashier."

Virgil waved it away. "You can find twerps like that anywhere. The main thing is, these big city banks are loaded to the gills with ready cash. Kansas City grows millionaires like Stockton grows wheat."

"How much you figure we'll get?" asked Boyd.

"A hundred thousand easy. More."

Boyd grinned, pushed his glasses up his nose. "Well, hell, what are we waiting for?"

"Planning," said Virgil. "Good, clear planning. Especially the getaway. You never know when they're gonna be tearing up streets."

"You mean case it?" asked Alex.

"Case the bank, case the town. Everything."

Hazel came in from the kitchen, carrying a tray loaded with sandwiches. Virgil stopped her from setting it down on top of the map. "Not now, huh?" She shrugged and laid it across the arms of a nearby overstuffed chair. Boyd snatched a chicken salad sandwich off the top of the pile as the tray went by. "Thanks, Hazel," he said, and bit into it. Hazel left the room.

"All right," said Virgil, removing his jacket. "First thing we're gonna do is get guns. I'm sick of paying a bill and up on each damn cork pistol we get from that jerk in Oklahoma City."

"The police station?" mumbled Boyd through a mouthful of chicken salad.

Virgil smiled. "The police station."

On the way up to Kansas City, the Ballard Gang, as it was now being called by the sensation-hungry press from the border of Mexico to the tip of Maine, stopped off to rob the Walker Police Department. There were only three policemen on duty at the time, and they were so busy playing pinochle at the back of the tiny station house that they didn't even notice the visitors until they had gotten the drop on the officers with their rented weapons. As a result, Virgil, Boyd, and Alex Kern walked out a few minutes later with three new machine guns, two sawed-off shot-guns, a Browning automatic rifle, two Lugers equipped with special thirty-one-shot magazines, a case of .45-caliber ammunition — and one bullet-proof vest. It was Boyd who insisted upon lugging it along, accompanied by a chorus of cursing on Virgil's part. They abandoned the Plymouth, too identifiable, in the next county and stole a snappy new red-and-white DeSoto for the drive into Kansas City.

Chapter Fourteen

The Kansas City First National occupied the first floor of a lofty fourteen-story structure just off Main Street. It was a conservative establishment, set off by an imitation marble pillar on either side of the revolving door, and marked by its name tastefully chiseled into the concrete lentil atop them. The Depression had made its presence known in the staggered pattern of shaded and darkened windows that studded the side of the building Each represented the corpse of another dead business.

The three newcomers sat unspeaking in the DeSoto parked across the street, silently watching the swarm of people hurrying in and out through the revolving door. Virgil struck a match on the wooden steering wheel and lit a cigarette. "Busy, isn't it?"

"That it is," agreed Alex gravely. "We're gonna

need an extra man behind the wheel, 'cause there's no way just the three of us is gonna rob that bank."

"I figured that before we left Stockton. That's why I called a guy recommened by a buddy of mine in McAlester. He lives here in K.C. Name's Roscoe Hunter.

"What's he done?"

"My buddy says he used to hijack beer trucks for the Capone mob."

Boyd Harriman whistled from the back seat. "That's some qualification."

"Yeah, but what's he done since? Capone's in stir two years now." The long drive had irritated Alex.

Virgil dragged on his cigarette and blew the smoke curling out the open window at his elbow. "Oh, he went legit for a while. Raced cars someplace in Indiana. Don't know what he's doing now."

"Any guy who's good enough to race in Indiana's good enough for me," said Boyd. "Where is he?"

"I got the address," said Virgil, starting the engine. "First I got to find a phone and let Hazel know we're here." He released the brake and drove off.

Hazel said goodbye to Virgil and hung up the receiver. She was seated on the couch with the flowered slipcover, her legs curled beneath her, a magazine lying open on her lap . . . a ten-cent New York detective quarterly, fresh from the Stockton drugstore.

It had been an empty conversation on both sides. Virgil had avoided mention of the upcoming bank robbery, though she had heard them planning it the day after her wedding, and Hazel had not brought up the subject of the magazine. Now she studied it again more closely. There was a rotogravure portrait of Virgil, Lansing Prison number and all, at the top of the page, and beneath it a bold offer of $5000 for any information leading to his arrest. This was standard. It was the facing page that had grabbed and held Hazel's attention. Here, a flattering picture of a stocky, distinguished-looking man occupied a spot in the center of a bold-faced article. The caption beneath identified the man in the photo as J. Edgar Hoover, Director of the Division of Investigation of the Department of Justice. The Feds were after Virgil Ballard.

Roscoe Hunter strode into the hotel room as if expecting a standing ovation. He was a medium-sized fellow with square shoulders and a toothy smile. He wore a long overcoat of some expensive material. Hatless, his thick hair tumbled in shiny black curls over his forehead. He drew an ivory comb from his coat pocket and ran it swiftly through these, smoothing them into symmetrical waves running straight back from his forehead. "Wet out there," he commented, jerking his thumb back toward the door.

Virgil looked up sharply from the damaged Luger magazine with which he was fiddling. He was sitting cross-legged on the thin flowered carpet, gun parts scattered around him. "Where the hell have you been?" he demanded. "I told you to be here by ten. It's half-past eleven."

"What's the hurry? We don't have to be there till one. Hiya, Boyd." He clapped a hand on Boyd's shoulder, making him drop the machine gun recoil spring he was holding. He caught it before it rolled off the table.

"It would be nice if we could drive past the bank a couple of times and figure out a good escape route, just in case the cops decide we're worth chasing." Virgil's voice was savage in its sarcasm. He rammed the vertical clip into the handle of the pistol. It protruded seven inches below the grip. "Where's that other Luger?"

Alex Kern reached into a compartment of the steamer trunk standing open in the center of the room and drew out a gleaming blue automatic, which he handed to Virgil. The gang leader picked up the second clip and began loading it from the square box of 9mm. ammunition beside him on the floor. "Verne Wilson said you was hot stuff in Chicago. I'm beginning to wonder. What'd Capone say when you showed up an hour and a half late for the St. Valentine's Day Massacre?"

"Aw, Virgil, I told you I didn't have nothing to do with that. I was strictly a hijacker."

"How are you on speed?" Alex wanted to know.

Roscoe shrugged. "I can handle sharp turns at eighty. After that I can't make guarantees.

"Yeah. Well, we damn well better be getting some guarantees before long. I'm sick of all this poor planning." Virgil got to his feet, jammed one of the assembled Lugers into his belt, and buttoned his vest over it. The overlong clip bulged beneath the material. "Boyd, Alex, ready?"

Boyd gave the actuating lever on the drum of his machine gun three fast twists and got up from the table. "I'm ready."

Alex slipped into his jacket. The shoulder holster he wore was effectively hidden beneath it. "Yeah, let's go." He clapped his hat on his head and grabbed his machine gun from its resting place against the wall.

"How's the weather?" Virgil fired the question at Roscoe Hunter.

Roscoe hesitated for a second before answering. "Just quit raining. Pavement's gonna be hell on driving."

"Good enough," said Virgil. "Break out the slickers."

Alex and Boyd went to the narrow closet and each took out a heavy raincoat and put it on. Alex's was a brown trench coat that, when buttoned up and buckled about the waist, hung down in sharp pleats just below his hips. The one Boyd had on was a simple oilcloth slicker, the kind Buster Crabbe wore in his Joe College movies, and swept around his knees. It was a shade darker than the gray cloth cap he had pulled low over his glasses, but that didn't matter because Boyd was not as clothes-conscious as Alex. Both coats were ideal for concealing machine guns.

Roscoe, who understood the purpose of the apparel, turned to Virgil and appraised his tan suit. "Where's yours?" he asked.

"I don't need one," said Virgil, smiling and patting the odd-shaped bulge beneath his vest. "No tommy gun."

"What good is that popgun if you got to shoot someone? What if you miss?"

"I won't miss." Virgil checked his wristwatch. "Okay, let's pull out."

Boyd said, "Hold it," and hurried across the room, stripping off his slicker as he went. "I almost forgot." He stopped at the open trunk and lifted out the heavy bulletproof vest. It took him a moment to figure out the complicated system of straps and buckles, then he slid his arms into it and strapped it on.

Virgil swore. "What are you doing?" Leave that sissy vest here!"

"It ain't sissy," insisted the youngster. "Cops always go for the guy with the machine gun. I'm not taking any chances here in cop city if I can help it." He straightened with difficulty, and pulled the raincoat on over the bulky vest.

"Jesus!" snorted Virgil. "Late wheel men and sissy vests!"

A few minutes later, the bank robbers were all seated in the red and white sedan, Alex Kern and Boyd Harriman, machine guns across their laps, in back, Virgil and Roscoe Hunter up front, Roscoe behind the wheel. "A DeSoto!" Roscoe exclaimed. "Classy, but ain't it a little . . . ah . . . conspicuous? For what we're doing, I mean?"

Virgil shook his head. "Nobody notices automobiles. By the time we're a block away from the heist, it'll be everything from a dark green Hudson to a bright yellow Essex with red spoke wheels. It's the guy driving that counts. So drive."

Roscoe started the engine, released the clutch, and the car lurched forward with a squeak of tires. "I just hope this thing is as hot as it looks," he said, and wheeled it into traffic.

When they got to the bank, they discovered a big green unmarked van parked before the entrance, its back doors hanging open and a stack of clean white lumber protruding over the bumper. A red flag flapped from the end of the longest board. "That ain't no armored car," observed Roscoe.

"Must be making repairs," said Virgil. "Drive around the block; maybe it'll be gone when we get back."

Roscoe accelerated and drove to the next intersection, then turned right. Traffic in the bank's vicinity was building up toward the rush hour. Motorists guided their vehicles carefully down the wet pavement, their tires skirting the broad standing puddles and sending droplets out in a fan-shaped pattern across the gutters. Other cars were parked bumper-to bumper beside the curb, some of them jammed into tight spaces so that their rear ends angled out into the street. Roscoe steered the DeSoto around these, cursing as he did so. "Some people should never be allowed behind the wheel of a car," he said through clenched teeth.

Virgil pointed out a side street to the right. "That street leads straight out of the business district. We can hit that after the heist and head north."

"What if we're tailed?" asked Alex from the back seat.

"Roscoe here'll shake 'em," said Virgil, and slapped the driver on the knee. "Won't you, Roscoe?"

"Well, like I said, no guarantees."

They turned and came abreast of the bank once again. The van was still there. "What now?" said Roscoe. "There's no place to park."

"Double-park it next to the van." Virgil studied the busy bank entrance.

"What if a cop comes along?"

"We'll worry about the cops."

"Yeah, but what'll I do if they tell me to move the car?"

"Move it."

Roscoe slid the car in next to the van and set the brake. Virgil swung open his door and put one foot on the running board. Then he turned to the driver. "Keep the motor running. If a cop comes anywhere near the bank, touch the horn three times, fast. Lightly. If they find out you're here, we're all dead. Got it?"

Roscoe nodded vigorously.

"Okay, c'mon." The order was snapped to Boyd and Alex in the backseat. They gathered their weapons and got out on both sides, Boyd having difficulty because of the heavy vest. Then they stepped between the battered van and a two-year-old Packard eight parked in front of it and mounted the low steps to the entrance.

Virgil was first through the revolving door, his thirty-one-shot Luger held out in front of him. Then came Alex and Boyd, machine guns cradled, and spread out on both sides of the entrance. The bank was full of people.

"This is a stickup," announced Virgil loudly. "Everybody get their hands in the air and nobody'll get hurt."

A woman customer began screaming and couldn't stop. Some of the customers near Virgil made a dash for the door, but Boyd's machine gun stopped them.

In his low cap and big raincoat open to reveal the quilted vest, he looked extremely menacing. They backed away from him, hands raised.

Virgil pointed his Luger at the pretty stenographer who sat petrified behind her little desk near the door, and waved it in the direction of the others huddled along the left wall. "You. Over there."

The girl sprang to her feet and fled across the room, high heels clacking on the checkerboard floor.

"Cut out that damn squawking!" Virgil swung the gun in the direction of the screaming woman. She couldn't stop. A little, gray-suited man at her side, probably her husband, clamped a hand over her mouth and choked it off.

The bank president, a man in his forties with graying hair and a small moustache, stood behind the varnished wooden gate that closed off his cubicle, hands held so high that the sleeves of his expensive jacket had slid down almost to his elbows. Two beefy forearms and the striped material of his shirt were exposed. "Open the vault," said Virgil, stepping through the gate. The president hastened to comply, leading the way around in back of the tellers' cages toward the enormous round vault door recessed into the rear wall. They passed a group of workmen clad in overalls, who had stopped their work on the half-finished pine partition they were building between the cages and the president's cubicle in order to raise their hands. "What's going on here?" said Virgil, pausing before a carpenter with a large paunch that hung over where his belt would have been if he had been wearing one.

"They're doing some remod —" began the bank

president, but Virgil cut him off by jabbing his gun at him.

"I was asking *him*." Virgil glanced at the man with the paunch, expecting an answer.

The workman said shakily, "We're puttin' a wall 'twixt the tellers an' the president."

"How come?"

"*He* ordered it." The carpenter nodded at the executive.

"What's the matter?" demanded Virgil, turning back to the president. "You figure maybe you're too good to associate with your employees? You're better than they are?"

The president stared at the gun the robber was pointing at his groin. "That's not true," he protested. "It's only to provide some privacy —"

"Privacy! Hah!"

"— Provide some privacy for the bank's customers. Savings accounts are very personal things, one must protect confidences —"

Virgil said, "I don't like it. Tear it down."

The carpenters stared at him, blinking.

"Didn't you hear me? I said tear it down!" He pointed the gun at the workmen.

Alex said, "Aw, Virgil, for Christ's sake —"

"Shut up!" snapped the other, and planted the muzzle of his Luger in the bank president's soft stomach. The executive grunted. "Now, if you bastards don't start tearing down that goddamn un-American partition by the time I count three, I'm gonna blast this man's guts all over the back wall. One!"

The carpenters snatched up their tools and began working furiously at the unfinished wall, wrenchingly tearing the clean white boards from the frame. Nails screeched and wood splintered as a particularly ambitious workman scurried along the partition, slamming his claw hammer into the bottom of the boards and loosening them, unmindful of the damage he was doing. The hammer blows reverberated like gunshots around the highceilinged lobby.

When the destruction was well under way, Virgil stood back and smiled with satisfaction. "That's more like it," he said, and spun the bank president around so that he could place his gun barrel against the man's spine. "Okay, you capitalist swine, the vault." He marched him toward the big steel door.

Out in the car, Roscoe Hunter had just snapped off the radio when he heard the hammer blows resounding from inside the bank and thought they were gunshots. He sat up straight, heart pounding, and stared toward the entrance through the side windows of the van beside which he was parked. Fifteen seconds went by, then, thirty and nobody came out the door. After a full minute, he figured the entire gang had been killed or captured. The motorcycle cop puttering up the street toward him confirmed it. He had been sent out to pick up the wheel man.

Roscoe released the hand brake and slammed his foot down on the accelerator. The car lurched, the engine coughed and died. He started it again and took off, this time successfully. The big DeSoto left the curb in a flurry of squealing rubber and roared down the street right past the motorcycle cop, fishtailing wildly on the slick wet asphalt. It barreled around the corner on two wheels and was gone.

The motorcycle patrolman stopped and turned in

his seat as the two-toned bomb sped past, and wondered what was going on. The bank was just up the street, on the left. He decided to go in there and check it out, just in case.

Inside the bank, the president fiddled with the big combination knob on the vault, his hand shaking so badly that his fingers kept sliding off.

"Come on, you fat bastard, hurry it up." Virgil kept jabbing him with his gun.

"I'm trying," protested the president. "I'm nervous. I keep going past the number."

"Well, get it. You want to foul up our neat schedule?"

Something inside the door went clunk and it swung open. "All right, step aside," directed Virgil, and put one foot into the vault. He pulled a black cloth sack from his pocket and glanced back across the bank floor. "Alex, get the cash out of the tellers' drawers. Boyd, make sure nobody gets cute." He began scooping money into the sack. Alex vaulted the marble counter and started in rifling the cash drawers while Boyd moved in to block the doorway, crouching over his machine gun, eyes eerily neutral behind the clear lenses of his big glasses.

"You're Virgil Ballard, ain't you?" The question, coming from somewhere in the crowd of hostages, was so unexpected that everything came to a complete stop.

Virgil paused to look at the crowd. "Who said that?" He studied the frightened faces.

An old farmer in a faded plaid shirt and clean overalls stirred in the center of the crowd. "I seen your pitcher in the paper. It's you, ain't it?"

Virgil hesitated, then grinned brightly. "Yeah, pops. Its me."

"I knowed it was you, yes, sir. Hee-hee." The farmer was almost jumping. "You're Public Enemy Number One, ain'cha?"

"That's what they say. Now shut up. I got work to do." He stooped and resumed filling his sack.

"Jesus Christ!" It came from the front of the bank, almost a scream.

Virgil stood ramrod-straight. Alex paused in his emptying of the cash drawers to see what was going on. Boyd, the one who had shouted was standing kitty-corner to the revolving door, staring past the glass panel, where a motorcycle cop was coming up the steps toward the bank's entrance.

"What the hell happened to Roscoe?" Virgil started to ask, but was cut off by Boyd's machine gun.

Boyd crouched almost to a kneel, clamped his gun to his hip, and cut loose. The glass in the door exploded outward. Bullets struck the wooden frame and the door began spinning. The cop catapulted backward as if he had been hit in the stomach with a baseball bat, a huge smear of blood slinging from his front and splattering across the marble steps, his cap sliding down his face and striking the bottom of the door frame, from which it bounced and rolled across the lobby floor. His head snapped back with the impact and he went over backward in a half sommersault. He landed at the bottom of the steps, his smashed head splatting against the sidewalk.

The door hadn't stopped spinning when the alarm bell began to clang. One of the tellers had hit the nearest switch and scampered back to where the rest of the employees were standing, watching the blood-spattered wreckage of the door in awe-struck silence. At the same instant, the bank president attempted to swing the heavy vault door shut while Virgil was inside. It struck his leg and he roared, smacking it so hard with the heels of his hands that it sprang back and narrowly missed clapping the president full in his distinguished face. As it was, he barely leaped back in time, and kept on moving as Virgil leveled his Luger and fired point-blank at him. Bullets streamed from the barrel like those of a machine gun, brrrrrping past the executive's ear as he belly-flopped to the floor. Every one of them missed.

Thinking he'd killed him, Virgil snatched his half-filled sack from the vault floor and loped toward the smashed bank entrance, taking the counter at a leap. Alex was right on his heels, his own sack lying forgotten beneath the open cash drawers as he galloped across the tile floor holding his machine gun like a balancing rod, horizontal across his midriff. "Hope you guys get away," called the old farmer as they dashed past. The alarm bell banged away relentlessly.

Boyd, who had remained crouching long seconds after the policeman's body had come to a rest on the sidewalk, came out of his trance and ran a close third behind Alex as he followed Virgil out the door.

There were cops all over the street. A few had come at the sound of the alarm. Most of them, however, were answering the silent alarm that had begun ringing in the police station the moment the three had entered the bank. Black-and-white patrol cars, their red lights flashing, were parked near the curbs, on the sidewalks, in the middle of the street, as were a number of official-looking motorcycles. The shot policeman lay in an impossible position at the foot of the steps that led up to the bank's entrance, his front torn open, his face shot away. The sidewalk all around him was stained dark with blood.

The cops started the shooting. Firmly entrenched behind their cars, they began firing the moment the bank robbers bolted into the open. Boyd and Alex gripped their machine guns tightly and sent twin streams of lead fanning out from the entrance, sweeping the exposed street. Bullets thumped and smacked and clanged into the parked cars, smashed windows and mirrors, chipped across brick buildings, zinged off the concrete sidewalks. Virgil, who had leaped sideways off the steps after his dash through the door, stood in the shelter of the lofty pillar that supported the ornate porch roof, firing short bursts from his converted Luger at the bluetopped heads that appeared for an instant above the roofs of the automobiles, then disappeared. The two machine guns were hammering away above his head. Every now and then, a deluge of ejected brass shell casings came raining down around him, but he ignored them and continued firing. While it was obvious from the level of his partners' fire that they were only trying to keep the cops busy, Virgil was shooting to kill.

"Boyd! Alex! The car!" Hunching low and depressing the trigger for a continuous burst, he began moving forward in the direction of the carpenters' van. Boyd and Alex came slowly down the steps, throwing lead at a steady rate over the officers' heads.

The lead was coming so furiously now that the police were trapped behind their cars, unable to move except to poke their heads into the open to take pot shots at the robbers, then duck back again as a new blast came their way. Virgil and Boyd and Alex came across the sidewalk like a small army, steadily advancing through the opposing fire, making their way toward and around the parked cars in an effort to get to the other side of the van. The only trouble was, when they got there, the DeSoto was gone. There was an empty space where they had left it, marked by two black streaks of rubber.

"Where the hell is Roscoe?" screamed Virgil, standing in the middle of the vacant street.

The police seemed to sense their predicament, for the fire from both sides of the street immediately stepped up. Orange flame erupted from all sides, plucking at the pavement around the stranded robbers, slamming holes into the "No Parking" signs at head level. One of the front tires of a police car near Alex Kern exploded and the car settled into a lopsided kneel. He retaliated with a new burst in the direction of the bullet's origin.

Boyd Harriman leaped to the curb opposite the bank and, in the middle of the deadly crossfire, poked his head through the open window of a parked automobile in search of the keys. There were none. Waddling awkwardly beneath the weight of his bulletproof vest, he scurried along the curb, checking every car on down the line, without success. He ducked down again.

Virgil exhausted his clip, threw it away, and slammed in a new one from his belt. He racked in a shell and began firing again, turning around and around as the opposing gunshots sounded near him. Alex, whose submachine gun had jammed momentarily, got it going again and raked across the already shattered car windows with short bursts.

Virgil was the only one with a comfortable amount of ammunition left. Alex and Boyd had come out with only their fifty-round drums and no extras, and these were getting low. Alex had taken to firing less than six bullets at a time, and Boyd, who was getting farther and farther away in his search for a suitable escape vehicle, wasn't firing at all at the moment. Only Virgil, the leader, was daring to rip away at the police with sustained bursts from his machine pistol. He came closer to exhausting his supply with each passing second. Save for Boyd, who had downed the motorcycle cop with his first hail of lead, nobody had hit anyone.

Then, from up the street, the answer came rolling smack into the middle of the action. A battered old Essex appeared at the top of the slight rise above the bank, its driver cheerfully oblivious to the inferno that had been going on for over twenty minutes. It bounced and jostled and shuddered right into the crossfire. Only when the big square windshield was shot away did the man in the driver's seat realize what was going on. He piled out, a white-haired old man in a cloth cap and worn tweed suit, and sprawled across the gutter, holding his hat and head down as the bullets whistled close over his head. The Essex, its motor still running, went on rolling down the street, in spite of the projectiles smacking into and through its doors, seats, wheels, windows, heading inexorably in the direction its absent driver had chosen.

Alex and Virgil spotted the abandoned vehicle at the same time and made a dash for it, firing all the way. Virgil ducked through the open door on the driver's side and grabbed the wheel while Alex, running alongside the moving car, clawed open the rear door on the passenger's side and threw himself headlong across the back seat. He scrambled to his knees and smashed the butt of his machine gun through the riddled back window, then switched ends and began firing through the hole in long, sweeping bursts,

Virgil, who had quit shooting long enough to yank the car into control, caught sight of Boyd Harriman in the rear-view mirror and shouted "Boyd! Come on!"

Thirty yards up the street, Boyd looked up from the parked car he was investigating and saw the bullet-scarred Essex rocking away down the street. Alex Kern leaning out the back window, machine gun blazing. Hugging his own weapon, he left the curb and hot-footed it down the middle of the thoroughfare in the direction of the escaping vehicle.

Alex spotted the youngster and redirected his fire so that he wouldn't hit him, hammering more bullets into the hissing vehicles parked by the curb. Out of the corner of his eye, he glimpsed the unmistakable blue of a policeman's uniform pop into the open on the other side of the street. A clear shot, if he were free to make a clean sweeping blast in the cop's direction, which he wasn't. In order to avoid cutting down Boyd, he was forced to chop off his fire and slide the gun in an arc toward the cop, then resume shooting at the uniform. The maneuver took too much time.

Boyd was running at top speed, his long slicker flowing out behind him, the weight of his bulletproof vest pulling him forward into a crouch. He was holding his machine gun out in front, flinging short bursts at the main body of lawmen on the side of the street opposite the bank. He didn't notice the cop bearing down on him from the other direction.

The cop, a foot patrolman who had just arrived on the scene, had his revolver out and, spotting the man in the bulletproof vest running toward him, snapped off three quick shots in his direction. Two of them struck Boyd in vest, knocking him off balance and putting holes in the fabric through which the shiny steel showed. The third grazed his shoulder. He was just in the act of dodging around the rear end of a poorly parked car when they hit, leaning at a precarious angle, one foot in the air. He scrabbled to regain his balance, his foot slipped on the slick pavement, the weight of the damaged vest pulled him over. A volley of shots came at him from the other side while he was in midair. Alex watched as the bullets struck Boyd from all sides, making his body dance in the air, smashing him in the legs, arms, face, jaw, and neck. A bullet crashed into the frame of his eyeglasses at the nose and they parted, falling in two sections from his head. He went down on his side and his machine gun leaped from his hands and bounced and rolled down the gutter. It came to a rest against the tires of a demolished police car. Alex's shoulders sank. "Step on it," he told Virgil half-heartedly.

Virgil, who had seen most of the action in the rear-view mirror, banged the shifting lever into third and punched the accelerator. The engine answered readily enough and the car lurched into a roar, speed-ing through the withering police crossfire. "I told him that damn vest was no damn good," he grumbled.

Alex kept up a steady return fire out the back window until the ammunition in his drum was exhausted. Then he dropped the machine gun bounc-ing on the seat beside him and drew his .45 automatic from his shoulder holster, with which he began snap-ping wild shots here and there at the rapidly receding police cars. The air was whooshing in cold through the empty windshield frame. The car hit a slick spot, throwing Alex hard against the doorpost as Virgil fought the steering wheel and bought the Essex skid-ding sideways around the corner. Then he accelerated again and the chaotic street fire was left behind. Alex slumped down in the back seat and put away his pistol. "I wonder what happened to Roscoe?"

"I don't know," said Virgil veering into the side steet they had chosen earlier and heading north. "But I sure as hell know what's *going* to happen to him." He forced the gas pedal down to the floorboards.

Long seconds after the shooting had stopped, the old man who had abandoned his car to the fugitives lay facedown in the gutter where he had fallen, hands clamped over his head. Then, slowly, as the strange new silence gave way to shouts and the sound of running feet, he raised his head, looked around, and pushed himself painfully up off the street, brushing dirt, water, and bits of glass from his soiled suit. Uniformed police officers were running all about him, some, like himself, showing signs of having spent a long time off their feet, the knees of their blue trousers dirty and worn. They all had guns in their hands.

The street in front of the bank was a shambles. Automobiles were parked everywhere; on the sidewalks, along the curb, straddling the center lane, their doors and windows and headlights shot full of holes, leaning at crazy angles on their blown tires, gasoline leaking from their pierced tanks, steam gushing from their smashed radiators. A few of the officers were seated behind the wheels of their damaged patrol cars, grinding away at the starters in fruitless attempts to get their cracked engines running. A motorcycle patrolman cursed and strained as he tried to push his overturned vehicle back onto its two wheels.

The old man stopped to look down at the body lying in a contorted position at his feet. Like the policeman who lay sprawled at the foot of the bank steps a few yards away, the dead man's face had been shot to pieces. Bits of flesh and bone splinters were stuck to the blood-splattered bulletproof vest just beneath his chin. His cap had slid down so that most of his torn features were mercifully concealed, and the old man didn't care to pick it up and see any more. He looked so young.

The foot patrolman whose revolver shots had thrown the bank robbers off balance and into the path of his comrades' fire in the first place came over to see the body. He glanced down at the half-hidden face, looked over in the direction of the slain motorcycle cop, and spat on the bullet-proof vest. Then he turned and was sick all over his shoes.

Chapter Fifteen

"The largest manhunt in the history of Missouri is under way today for Virgil Ballard, the infamous Tri-State Terror, who, with six members of his gang, robbed the First National Bank of Kansas City yesterday afternoon, slaying Officer Malcolm Jackson and escaping with an undetermined amount of cash. The pitched battle raged for twenty-seven minutes, during which —"

Virgil snapped off the radio of the freshly stolen Auburn and pulled out to pass a slow-moving Model T produce truck. He left it behind in a swirl of dust from the pavement. "Undetermined amount of cash! You hear that? They can't count a lousy twelve thousand." He steered back into the right lane, just missing a head-on collision with a big Franklin going in the other direction. The angry driver gave him a blast with his air horn.

"Yeah," agreed Alex, after his heart had started beating again. "They got the number of the gang wrong too."

"They didn't even mention Boyd."

"You didn't give them a chance."

Virgil stared at the road for a minute. Then he looked at Alex. "You figure they killed him?"

"Yeah."

They came in view of a bicyclist pedaling down the edge of the road in the same direction they were going. He was wearing an argyle jersy and knickers, and wore a cap at a cockeyed angle that left the bill low over his left eye. He turned his head, saw them, and wheeled closer to the edge. Virgil accelerated and shot past him, so close that the cyclist panicked, twisting the handlebars too quickly, and tipped over. Alex craned his neck around to watch him through the rear window. The rider and the vehicle were tangled together, the two upturned wheels spinning away at the empty air.

"Now what did you go and do that for?" Alex wanted to know.

"Don't like two-wheelers," Virgil answered.

"Look, Virge, why don'cha pull off to the side so we can take a nap?"

"What for? I'm not sleepy."

"I am."

"So sleep. Who's stopping you?"

"I'm afraid I might not wake up again. Look, why the hurry?"

Virgil shot the car straight past the upcoming curve

and onto a narrow gravel road, kicking up a cloud of yellow dust. "I got my eye on a bank in Oklahoma. I wanna hit it before noon."

"Another one?" Alex's eyes opened wide. "After what just happened?"

"So we hit some hard luck. That don't mean we should give up robbing altogether, does it?"

"On the level. Why another one so soon after the last one? We got enough to live on for a while."

"I want to get together enough so we can lay up for a long stretch."

"Then what?"

Virgil clenched his teeth. "Then I'm gonna come back to Missouri and kill Roscoe Hunter." He rumbled on down the road, trailing a ribbon of brown dust and gravel.

Roscoe Hunter trotted down the steps of the building where he kept his apartment in Kansas City, tossed his heavy brown suitcase into the back seat of the DeSoto, got into the driver's seat, and drove off. The radio, which he had left on when he parked the car, warmed up and the announcer's doomsday voice thundered from the round speaker: " . . . pitched battled raged for twenty-seven minutes, during which gang member James Boyd Harriman lost his life to the merciless justice of the Kansas City Police. Virgil Ballard and the rest of his gang escaped in a stolen vehicle belonging to Ralph Budge, 76, of Independence. More news following this message of interest from Bristol-Meyers, makers of —"

Roscoe fumbled the knob to the "off" position with shaking fingers. There was nothing new in the message, only additional means for panic. He'd known about Virgil's escape ever since late yesterday afternoon, after he'd gotten home and received the evening edition of the newspaper. That's when he'd begun packing.

He'd have been gone hours earlier if it had not been for the police. The streets near his apartment house had been alive with patrol cars all evening, their sirens piercing the night air, their side-mounted spotlights sweeping the darkened windows of every building on the block. Roscoe, not realizing that the motorcycle patrolman who had seen him speeding away from the bank was the one who'd been slain, was afraid that the police would have his licence number and that they'd converge upon him the moment he struck out with the DeSoto. This morning, however, after a sleepless night, he'd decided to chance it. There was no predicting what that crazy Ballard would do once he found out that his wheel man had panicked and left him in the lurch.

Now, as he drew farther and farther from his apartment house and nothing of consequence occurred, he relaxed a little. With the remission of fear came logic. He began to make plans, to formulate a destination for what had started out as a headlong flight from danger. He'd head north to Illinois, or maybe farther, all the way to Michigan. There, he could set himself up in business as an auto mechanic or something of the sort, change his name, start a new life. Small chance of the "Tri-State Terror" venturing that far from the safety of his native region for purposes of mere vengeance. Yes, things were looking up.

Then he heard the sirens.

A police car came squealing around the corner just as Alex and Virgil were leaving the bank in Claremore, Oklahoma. Virgil socked the sack full of cash into the back seat and followed it in, while Alex, nearest the driver's side, slid beneath the wheel, starting the engine, and tore off from a standing start.

Close behind, the officer on the passenger's side leaned out the window and snapped off a few shots that whistled past the Auburn, one of them clipping the left-hand mirror and knocking it crooked. Virgil crunched the butt of a submachine gun through the back window, jammed the barrel through the ragged hole, and began firing long sweeping bursts at windshield level. He shot high and took out a line of store windows along the right side of the street.

The main street intersection was coming up. Alex accelerated and ran the red light. A car coming from the right squealed its brakes and skidded around, narrowly missing a double-parked bus parked near the corner. The shaken driver leaned angrily on his horn. Behind them, the police car, siren wailing, shot between two other cars going in opposite directions across the intersection and sent them slewing around sideways to a symphony of tortured tires. Virgil raked a withering blast with his machine gun across the pursuers' radiator and missed. They zigzagged and fishtailed wildly across both lanes in an attempt to dodge bullets coming at them from the exposed policeman's gun, at the same time throwing off Virgil's aim so that he wasted ammunition on the empty air. "Quit screwing up and steer straight, damn you," he commanded.

"Not on your life!" Alex retorted, twisting the wheel so that the speeding car veered from one lane to the other, then twisting it back the other way.

Virgil cursed and braced himself on both knees, took careful aim at the pursuing car, and squeezed the trigger. The bullets ripped across the police windshield in a kaleidoscope of disintegrating glass. Immediately, the front end of the black-and-white vehicle twisted around, brought the rear arcing around in front, and walloped into the trunk of a huge elm tree planted in a square box on the left curb. As the scene grew smaller through the Auburn's back window, the police driver, unhurt, climbed out of the crippled vehicle and helped his shaken partner out onto the sidewalk. Virgil laughed and fired a final short burst in their direction, though by now they were well out of range.

Hazel was standing in front of the house outside Stockton when they drove up. She looked anxious, nervously twisting the rolled-up newspaper in her hands. Virgil set the brake and got out. "I heard the car coming down the road," she said when he joined her. "I hoped it was you."

What is it?"

She handed him the newspaper. He looked at her thoughtfully, then unrolled it.

Alex hefted the suitcase in which they had put the money out of the car. "Bad news?"

Virgil turned the paper so that Alex could read the headline:

GANG MEMBER TELLS ALL
Caught Driving Stolen Car
Ballard Man Spills Beans

Underneath was a picture of Roscoe Hunter.

"Sonuvabitch," said Alex, almost inaudibly.

"Put the suitcase back in the car," hissed Virgil solemnly.

Part IV

Mr. Henry

The Shawnee water tower is visible now in the distance, a black form pasted against the charcoal gray sky. Tiny pinpoints of light begin to blink on in scattered parts of the city's low profile. Darkness is beginning to lose its grip.

The folded shop awning above Sheriff McCracken's head bulges and releases a thin stream of rain water onto his Stetson. It rolls off the brim and runs onto his glistening leather jacket, mixing with the moisture left by the slowly receding December drizzle. He pays it no attention as he sweeps the beam of his flashlight around the inside of the shop through the plate window, then moves on.

Up ahead, Jake, the lanky deputy, searches a high old automobile parked by the curb. His light flashes around the front and back seats, the door slams with a thunk, and he turns his back on the car in favor of the nearby alley. McCracken hears the garbage cans rattle as he lifts and replaces the lids. If Ballard's hiding beneath a banana peel, he muses, Jake will find him.

Circles of light dance and dart along the walls of the buildings, inside and out, as the uniformed men comb the street on both sides. Several streets to the west, the persistent whooping of the hounds informs the sheriff of the federal agents' progress. Dogs, men, flashlights, guns. What do the papers call it? The Army of Justice.

A deputy on the opposite side of the street calls out. Slinging his shotgun to a two-handed grip, McCracken trots across.

The deputy hands him a gleaming brass cylinder about the size of a tie clip. "I found it on the sidewalk. It must of lodged in his pants cuff."

Sheriff McCracken examines the tiny casing in the light of his torch, turning it over between his fingers. "Nine millimeter," he says, his voice surprisingly calm. "Luger."

The darkened shop windows stare blankly back at them.

Chapter Sixteen

October 12, 1933.

She had light brown hair, cropped short so that it fell just below her ears, which were pierced but without earrings. She was, in fact, almost completely unadorned, her face plain, her yellow dress devoid of frills, shoes dusty and run down at the heels. The one concession she had made to ornament was a string of red beads the size of Ping-Pong balls she had hung around her neck. Tall, a bit gawky, shy to the point of being awkward, not pretty. Zazu Pitts in her younger days. Mrs. Alex Kern.

Virgil grinned and took her hand. It felt warm and damp. "How d'you do, Mrs. Kern? Annabelle, is it? I never woulda knowed ol' Alex had a wife if we didn't stop here for you. No sir." He winked at Alex.

The plain woman smiled a hesitant greeting, but said nothing.

"Annabelle and me, we got an understanding." Alex's smile was a bit strained. "She don't bore anybody bragging about me, I don't bore anybody bragging about her. Keeps friends friends."

Hazel and Virgil laughed politely. Annabelle smiled.

"Well, I guess I'll get my luggage." Her voice was faint, almost a whine. She stood there a minute awkwardly, then turned and headed down the flat stone walk toward the frame house. Some of its windows were boarded up and the peeling front door sagged on its sprung hinges.

"I'll help," said Hazel, and trotted off to join her.

When the door had clapped shut behind the women, Virgil lit a cigarette. "Where in perdition's flame did you find her?" The smoke curled from his parted lips.

"Family," answered Alex, leaning back on the fender of the gunmetal-colored Packard convertible Virgil had bought in Muskogee. His own vehicle, a new black Pontiac sedan he had stolen at the same time, was parked just behind it. "She's my cousin. I married her when I was seventeen."

"Why for chrissake? If you don't mind my saying so, Alex, she looks like a sparrow in moulting season."

Alex smiled. "Yeah, she does, don't she? Her pa, my uncle Mike, made me marry her. Claimed she was in a family way."

"Was she?"

Alex nodded. "What her pa didn't know was, she

seen a doc in Wisconsin when she was supposed to be visiting a relative. Got it fixed."

"She didn't tell him?"

"Nope."

Virgil reached out and snatched a curled brown leaf from the hood of the convertible. It crunched in his hand. "Well, if you don't like her, why are we taking her with us?"

"Oh, she's all right. Anyway, you said we'd be laying up for a long spell out West, so I figured I oughtta have a woman around, seeing as you got one."

"Hazel's different. I can pass the time with her."

Alex laughed shortly. "Don't let Annie's looks fool you. I don't know where she learned them things she knows, but she sure knows 'em."

"How much she know about you?" Virgil nodded at the Pontiac. "I'm not about to go sneaking them rifles and machine guns in and out of the house after she goes to sleep."

"Don't worry about her. Her brother's doing five to ten in Jeff City for armed robbery and her pa was in bootlegging in the '20s. She's been around our kind all her life. She won't give us a second thought."

"She better not."

Alex was about to ask him what he meant when Hazel and Annabelle, each carrying a suitcase, fumbled out the door of the shack and came toward them. Alex held out his hands to take their burdens, but Hazel shook her head. "Don't stand on ceremony, boys. We can hold up our own." She turned and headed for the sedan, Annabelle stumbling behind her beneath the weight of her own big suitcase.

"Well, at least let me open the door for you," said Alex, and hurried ahead of them, hand reaching for the doorhandle. Virgil followed, puffing on the butt of his cigarette.

Hazel loaded her burden onto the back seat of the sedan, took Annabelle's, and slid that in beside it. The barrels of two machine guns and an automatic rifle protruded plainly from beneath a thin flannel blanket on the floor behind the front seat. If she'd seen them, Annabelle didn't show it. Virgil grinned and snapped away his cigarette butt.

"All right," he said, "Alex you and Annie'll ride in the Pontiac. Me and Hazel get the coupe. Let's go." He put a hand on Hazel's arm to lead her toward the Packard.

"I sort of hate to leave the place." Annabelle stared across at the house, at its roof sagging in the middle like a swaybacked horse, at the carpet of fallen leaves covering the parched yard.

"Forget it," said Alex, slamming shut the sedan's back door. "It's a dump. The bank'll get it anyway."

"Pa gave it to me."

"I said forget it."

They stood a moment in silence, Virgil and Hazel and Alex watching Annabelle watch the house. "Well," said Virgil, stirring, "I guess we better go while it's still October." He raised his right hand in parting. "See you in Shawnee."

The rental agent shuffled the papers with his nicotine-stained hands and turned them so Virgil could sign the bottom line. Virgil bent over the coffee table, scrawled "Warren Henry," and sat back in the overstuffed couch.

"Well, I guess that's it, Mr. Henry." The agent slipped the papers into his open briefcase, snapped it shut, and stood up. He was a big, soft-looking easterner, with a thick neck around which his too-small shirt collar was buttoned painfully. "I hope you and Mrs. Henry like the place." He smiled at Hazel, who looked pretty and well scrubbed in her brick-colored suit and flowered hat. She smiled back.

"I'm sure we will, Mr. Emmett," said Virgil, getting up and shaking his hand. "And don't you worry about us living here. We're quiet folks, me and the missus, just looking for relaxation. My brother, too, and his wife."

"That's my client's lookout, not mine. But for my money, you're all good folks." The agent put on his hat, said good-bye and left.

After his car had driven off, Virgil walked around the room, circling the leaf-patterned carpet, admiring the high ceiling, lifting the drapes on the tall front window. "It's all ours, free and clear. Whaddaya think of it, babe?" He turned to face Hazel, who had joined him at the window, and took her hands in his.

"It's wonderful," she said calmly. "How long will this one last?" Her voice was ironic.

"Stop worrying. We got us a house right here in town, all legal, and thirty thousand dollars in our pockets. Well, twenty-eight. It'll last as long as we want it."

"That's what you said about Stockton."

Virgil slid his hat to the back of his head. "Stockton was no good from the start. In them small burgs, where everybody knows everybody else, strangers stick out like yeller cows. People notice things. Shawnee now, this is the place. Big enough to get lost in, little enough to get out of if you have to."

"Is that what makes a town good? Its escape possibilities?"

Virgil sighed, a little puzzled. "Well, you got to think of them things. Look, don't even give 'em a notion. Let me worry about that. And take off that hat. It makes you look like a prize horse." He lifted the flowered hat off her head, fumbling with the pin, and tossed it onto the couch.

"Thanks," Hazel said drily, "for the compliment."

"Oh, shut up," said Virgil, and crushed her to his lips.

"Break it up, you two." Alex, loaded down with suitcases, scrabbled though the front doorway with Annabelle on his heels. He set them down with a thud and straightened to look around the living room. "No, sir," he said, "not bad at all. I got to applaud your taste, Virge, if nothing else."

"You're cute." Virgil, his arm around Hazel, glared at him in mock anger.

"Like it sugar?" Alex draped his arm around his wife's shoulders.

"It's nice," she said.

"Nice? Beats the old shack all to hell."

Virgil said, "Put the Pontiac in the garage. We'll bring them guns in through the kitchen."

"Yeah, right." Alex went out the door, pausing

to give Annabelle a smart smack on the rump. She gasped.

There was a big floor-model radio in the corner with a shawl draped at an angle across its top. Virgil went over to it and turned it on. The tubes hummed. "I hope they get 'Amos 'n' Andy' out here."

"I hope they got country," Annabelle ventured. "I like country."

"Hell with country. Always somebody dying. What's the matter with this thing?" He slapped the side of the wooden cabinet. The tubes crackled and resumed humming.

"Give it time to warm up," suggested Hazel.

Music came crackling out the big square speaker. Virgil twisted the selector knob, found the right frequency, and stood back triumphantly. "Frankie Trumbauer," he said. "Used to listen to his orchestra all the time in McAlester."

Alex came in from the kitchen and laid his blanket-wrapped bundle on the couch. Barrels rattled. "All parked," he informed Virgil. "You gonna leave your buggy out front?"

"Why not? It's legal. Not like yours."

"Even so, Packards ain't that common around here. Attracts attention. There's a Depression, you know."

"Really? I haven't noticed."

"Anyway, I'd park her out back."

"Yeah. I'll do it later."

Alex tapped his foot to the music coming from the radio. "Hey, that's a catchy tune. Anybody want to dance?" He held out his hands.

Virgil grinned. "Go ahead, honey." He gave Hazel a gentle push. She smiled and stepped into Alex's arms. They began dancing around the room.

"Hey, Virge, you got a great dancer here."

"That's why I married her." Virgil looked at Annabelle, standing quietly off to one side. "Shall we?" She shook her head. He stepped up, seized her hands, spun her into his embrace, and steered her across the rug. She danced stiffly, with small, uneven steps, her smile frozen.

At the end of the walk in front of the neat white house, a small man in a tweed suit and narrow-brimmed hat stood watching the gay scene through the tall window. His creased face, flushed by the brisk autumn breeze was stern and disapproving. He was the owner of the house.

Chapter Seventeen

"Virge, what's the matter?" Alex, shirtsleeves rolled up past his elbows, looked up from the mass of tubes and wires with which he was fiddling on the inside of the big radio. The floor around him was littered with tools. The radio's pasteboard back leaned against the wall where he had placed it.

Virgil tossed him the folded newspaper. "Take a gander."

Alex ignored the scare headline, his eyes darting to the lead story on the right-hand side of the page.

> Haileyville, Oklahoma, November 17—A light snow was falling here today as five men, identified by witnesses as the infamous Ballard gang, charged into the Haileyville Savings & Loan Company, killing

a guard and escaping with an estimated $27,000 in cash and negotiable bonds.

According to Arthur Honeywell, the bank's president, four men came into the bank at 1:30 P.M., one of them armed with a machine gun, and demanded all the money in the teller cash drawers. A fifth man, he said, remained just outside the door with a sawed-off shotgun in his hands.

No sooner had the announcement been made than Franklin Peevey, 63, the guard, pulled his pistol from its holster and attempted to fire it at the bank robbers. The man with the machine gun shot him dead before he could pull the trigger.

The other three men proceeded to clean out the cash drawers and empty the contents into a cotton sack. This done, they backed out the door, got into their car, described by witnesses as a dark blue Hudson sedan, and drove off.

Honeywell described the machine gunner as "tall and blond, wearing a gray suit and hat," and sporting a pair of expensive-looking shoes. This description, police said, fits Virgil Ballard, Public Enemy Number One, who is wanted in Missouri, Kansas, and Oklahoma for crimes ranging from bank robbery to murder. Police also believe that the man at the door with the shotgun may have been Alex Kern, who, since helping Ballard escape

from the Oklahoma State Penitentiary at
McAlester two years ago, has been riding
with the Tri-State Terror.

Mrs. Alvina Peevy, the guard's widow,
was unavailable for comment.

Subject of the most massive manhunt
in the history of the Tri-State area, Virgil
Ballard. . . .

Virgil snatched the paper from Alex's hands before
he could read further. "How do you like that?" His
face was flushed an angry red.

"We sure are busy, ain't we?"

"Busy, hell!" Virgil dashed the paper to the floor
in a flurry of pages. "What do you think we're doing,
sitting around here twiddling our thumbs in this God-
forsaken nothing town? We're supposed to be laying
low until the papers lose interest in us. So now they
got us robbing a bank in Hailcyville, for God's sake!"

"I never thought that bank'd go for twenty-seven
thousand. Maybe we should of hit it."

"Didn't you read it?" We just did! 'Tall and blonde
. . . gray suit and hat!' That must fit a million guys
in Oklahoma alone. Why's it got to be me?"

"You do wear expensive shoes."

Virgil ignored him. "What the hell's the matter
with them damn cops, anyway? They ought to know
better than to tag something on me just because
a guy's tall and blond. Christ, they might as well
arrest Jimmy Cagney!"

"Cagney's not tall. Look, Virge, why let it get to
you? It's happened before."

"Yeah, but it's so damn unfair."

Alex picked up his screwdriver and used it to pry

straight the fitting on the bottom of the yellow glass tube he held in his hand. "Well," he said, "that's the price of fame, I guess."

Hazel came in from the kitchen, carrying a cut-glass bowl of fruit. She was wearing a gray dress and flowered apron, and had a thin sweater buttoned at the nape of her neck like a cape. "Where have you been?" she asked Virgil, setting the bowl on the coffee table.

"I went downtown to get that tire fixed." He took an apple from the bowl, felt it suspiciously, and rapped it on the edge of the table. It made a sharp knocking sound. "Wax." He tossed it disgustedly back into the bowl.

"Did you get a newspaper?"

"No." Virgil turned away.

Hazel bent down to pick up the tangle of pages on the floor. "Then what's this?" She straightened it out, found the front page and read it. Her expression was unchanged as she looked up from it. "Does this mean we have to leave?"

"No reason. It'll blow over." Virgil took the paper gently from her hands and placed it on the coffee table. "These punks who got to storm banks like they was forts don't last. The cops'll pick 'em up on their next job and the heat's off."

"They'll run a big investigation in the area."

"Wrong again. Haileyville's too close. The cops'll expect 'em to be hundreds of miles away from here by nightfall, and they'll be right. No crooks in their right minds would stick around after hitting for twenty grand."

"Except maybe us." Alex sat back on his heels and plugged the radio into the wall. The tubes glowed.

Virgil looked at him. "Yeah. Except maybe us."

Hazel said, "As long as we're talking about money, has anybody paid the rent lately? The landlord called about it yesterday."

"Let him stew," said Virgil. "The guy's a creep anyway, all that nut talks about is religion, fish-eyeing everything the minute he gets in the door."

"You think he suspects something?"

"Nah, I doubt if nuts like him even read the papers."

The dog began barking outside, loud and full-throated.

"That damn dog again," said Virgil, heading for the door. "I'll shut him up." He went out.

"He's nothing but a lot of trouble," Hazel said. "I don't know what you brought him here for, Alex. He eats more than any of us."

The radio hummed. "It's worth it for the protection we get. If any of them laws come around here, boy, we'll know it."

"I don't see how, the way he barks at every little noise, all the time. It could just as well be a screech owl as —"

The dog, a big spotted pointer, came bounding into the room and proceeded to smother Alex's face in wet kisses. "Easy, Josh. Down, boy." He slapped the dog reassuringly on the rib cage. Josh panted joyfully.

Virgil came in, brushing dog hairs off his jacket.

"We got to get him a new collar. He's almost wore the old one clean through."

"Another one?" Alex was astonished. "How's he do it?"

Annabelle came in, wearing a bathrobe and slippers, her hair tied up in an orange bandanna. The dog spotted her and ran toward her. She squealed and backed swiftly out of the room, slamming shut the door just as Josh planted his paws against the lower panels. He scratched at the door, whimpered, then gave up and returned to Alex, tail wagging.

"Come on out, hon," Alex called through the door. "He just wants to make friends."

"I'm not coming out till you get rid of that animal." Her voice was surprisingly strong.

"He won't even chase a cat. He's friendly."

"I'm not coming out till you get rid of that animal," she repeated.

Virgil made a growling noise in his throat. "Dogs, radio repairmen, women scared of animals. 'The Ballard Gang!'" He struck the door jamb with the heel of his hand.

"Hey!" exclaimed Alex, one ear clapped against the speaker. "Music! I think I fixed the radio!"

In his one-room bungalow on the other side of Shawnee, the landlord awoke to hear the news commentator's voice booming from the battered Philco atop the high-boy. He was seated in a low cane chair, his Bible lying open across his knees, marker ribbon hanging down from the spine. He had slept through the morning sermon, clean into the twelve o'clock news.

" . . . But legislators are confident of a quick victory. On the home front, the search for Public Enemy Number One Virgil Ballard has shifted to southern Kansas, where local police yesterday found abandoned the car believed to have been used by the Ballard Gang during the daring holdup of the Haileyville Oklahoma Savings and Loan Company last month. The car, a 1932 Hudson, was discovered in a farmer's field just outside of Lawrence, hidden beneath a pile of loose brush. It is registered to Alvin A. Christie, an Oklahoma cattle buyer who reported it stolen November 15.

"Virgil Ballard is thirty-two years old, stands six feet tall, weighs 170 pounds. He had blond hair and blue eyes, and has a small mole above his right elbow. He may be traveling with fellow bank robber Alex Kern, who is also six feet tall, weighs 159 pounds, has black hair and blue eyes. If you see either of these men, report it to your local police headquarters. They will send it on to the Division of Investigation in Washington, D.C. We pause here for a message from Woolworth's department store, who has something to say about your Christmas shopping list," the smooth voice droned.

The landlord got up and switched off the radio. Raindrops were beginning to tap at the window, swimming down the glass and collecting in tiny puddles on the sill outside. The landlord felt a chill, and drew on the ratted old sweater he had left draped over the back of the cane chair. "Six feet tall, blond hair, blue eyes, mole just above —" He came out of his lethargy and grasped the telephone from the end table, knuckles whitening on the upright cylinder as he dialed.

Chapter Eighteen

"Yes, sir. We certainly will, sir. Thank you, sir." The redheaded desk sergeant looked bored as he hung up the phone.

"Anything important?" The plainclothesman, leaning across the end of the wooden counter, looked up from his newspaper.

The sergeant shook his head, feigning a yawn. "Another Ballard sighting. Seems this guy rented a house to him on the South Side."

"Think there's something to it?"

"You got the paper. Long way between here and Lawrence, Kansas."

"Yeah." The detective turned to the funny pages. "I guess you're right."

It was drizzling steadily by the time the sun settled behind the jagged city skyline, its descent hidden by the thick cloud cover. Hazel, in a flowered dressing gown, was flinging handfuls of glittering tinsel onto the branches of the small Christmas tree Alex had brought home and set on the table before the tall front window. Annabelle was curled up on the couch reading a movie magazine. She was wearing the same bathrobe and slippers she'd had on the day the dog had chased her into the adjoining room. The radio was playing Christmas carols.

Hazel paused in her work to look out into the drooling rain. "Don't tell me Alex is still out walking that dog," she said.

"Maybe he stopped somewhere," suggested Annabelle, staring at a full-page shot of John Barrymore posing beside his custom-built automobile.

"Where?"

"Oh, a bar or something. Alex gets lonely at times."

Virgil came in from the master bedroom, hair mussed, shirttail hanging untidily outside his pants. "Damn music," he grumbled, flipping the radio off. "How's a guy supposed to get rid of a headache with all that going on?" He went into the kitchen, came back out before the door stopped swinging, a bottle of aspirins in one hand and a glass of water in the other. He downed two tablets, emptied the glass, and set the remains beside the pygmy tree. "I feel better already."

"You'd feel even better if you cut down on your drinking," said Hazel. She hung a shining red globe on one of the branches, bowing it almost to the level of the table.

"Says you. Where's the boy and his dog?"

"Still out."

"In that?" Virgil cupped his hands about his eyes so he could see out the window. "Christ, I hope he brought his night glasses with him."

"Annie says he might've stopped off at a bar."

Virgil turned to Annabelle. "What bar?"

Annabelle looked up from John Barrymore. "Any bar. Alex likes to get acquainted with bartenders."

"Yeah, I'll bet."

The door opened and Alex came in, raincoat streaming water. "Man! That ain't gonna let up tonight." He closed the door on the hissing rain.

"Where's the dog?" Hazel asked.

"I tied him up out front. He can take it."

"Stop anywhere?" Virgil wanted to know.

Alex slid out of the raincoat. "Yeah, at a saloon. Why?"

"What if it gets raided?"

Alex looked thoughtful. "Yeah. Hey, I never thought of that."

Virgil's eyes were hard. "Well, from now on, *think* about it." He flopped into a chair and fished a cigarette out of his pocket. "Any news?"

"Not much." Alex hung his coat on the hall tree. It dripped loudly on the raised floor before the door. "Oh, yeah, we're in Kansas. Cops found the car that bunch used in Haileyville, and that's where they're looking."

"Let 'em keep looking. Anything else?" Virgil lit his cigarette.

The other robber glanced suspiciously in the direction of the women. Annabelle was still engrossed in her magazine, and Hazel was adjusting the silver angel on the top of the tree. When Alex spoke, his voice was low. "I got us a bank."

Virgil appraised him in silence, squinting through his cigarete smoke. A long, low, whooping sound drifted into the room from the front yard. Virgil stirred in his seat. "There goes that damn dog again," he said.

The red-haired sergeant lifted the paper cup of coffee to his lips, then paused to remove the slip of paper which had adhered to the bottom, and set the cup back down untasted. It was the bulletin that had come in during his break, the one he had put aside to read later. He had forgotten about it until this moment. Now, five minutes before the end of his shift, he wondered if he should leave it for Sergeant Kirby, who would be taking over presently. If it were something important, however, the delay wouldn't look good on his record. He sighed and unfolded the missive.

As he read, his eyes widened. He snapped up the telephone, letting the report glide to the floor, and dialed the number of the Oklahoma headquarters of the Investigation Division of the Department of Justice. Kansas State troopers had apprehended the men who had abandoned the getaway car outside of Lawrence. Neither of them knew Virgil Ballard.

Virgil spread a map of Shawnee he had picked up at the neighborhood service station on the dining room table. Hazel had turned the radio back on, and Christmas carols slid underneath the closed door. He looked questioningly at Alex.

"Right here," said Alex, pointing out a narrow street near the river. "The Shawnee National. Set between a flophouse and a candy store. Cathouse across the street."

"Nice neighborhood."

"Listen, it's better than having a gunshop next door. You never know what these rubes are gonna do when they get a whiff of that reward money. Anyway, this is the biggest bank in town, and one of the largest in Oklahoma. There's gotta be, oh, ninety, a hundred thousand in that place on any given day."

Virgil looked doubtful. "They don't leave money like that laying around unguarded."

"Well, that's the catch. There are six regular guards in all, four in the lobby and two in the vault. Two of them are plainclothes. Also they got a guy stationed above the door with a tommy gun.

"What? No tank?"

Alex ignored the sarcasm. "The guys in uniform are easy. We can get the drop on them the minute we come through the door. Plainclothesmen are easy to spot, 'cause they look like cops, and we can grab them at the same time. The guards in the vault, we got them when it opens. Simple."

"And the guy with the chopper?"

"Window dressing. What's he gonna do, cut loose in a room full of innocent bystanders? I tell you,

Virge, this is gonna be an easy hundred grand. Then we can split up and get the hell away from the heat. Mexico maybe."

"We're gonna need more guys."

"I know a few of the local boys. They're dependable, and they know how to follow orders. Whattaya say?"

"I don't know. Let me think about it."

Alex straightened. "Okay, that's your privilege. But I wouldn't wait too long. Bank jobs rot just like everything else."

The rain-soaked scene outside the window was draped in the purplish black of late evening, leaving only the water-streaked glass for Virgil to contemplate. At last he stretched mightily, arching his body and driving his long arms straight toward the ceiling. "Mexico, huh?" he said, yawning. "What do you suppose it's like down there?"

It was nearly midnight by the time the lawmen in Oklahoma City had organized themselves for the trip to Shawnee. There were three big sedans lined up at the curb in front of federal headquarters, one of them a black-and-white sheriff's patrol car, the other two unmarked government vehicles. The damp night air was alive with the clicks and rattles of over a dozen firearms as their owners made last-minute checks of their weapons in the glare of the headlights. Pump shotguns rattled beside submachine guns, the breeches of assorted automatic pistols banged and slammed, their checked grips squeaking in the tense wet fists of their handlers, bulletproof vests were hefted gruntingly into the back seats of the first two cars. When the noises of preparation had died down, William Farnum turned to Sheriff McCracken and asked him how far they had to go.

"Forty-three miles. We ought to be there in three hours."

"Make it two," snapped the federal agent, and ducked into the back seat of the lead car. The sheriff glared.

Five minutes later, the caravan of heavy vehicles pulled out on the first leg of its forty-three-mile journey.

"Whose car we gonna use on this job?" Virgil, his shirt collar wilted and the knot of his tie hanging in the vicinity of his breast pocket, was sitting across the map-covered table from Alex, an ashtray overflowing with cigarette butts at his side. The mantel clock in the living room struck one.

Alex shrugged. "The Pontiac, I guess. Your job's still at the garage, ain't it?"

"Transmission trouble," replied Virgil. "In a brand-new car, not a hundred miles on it. How about that?"

"Yeah, Detroit's getting pretty careless. My car, then?"

The other nodded. "We'll probably need another one, too, what with more men going along."

"No problem. We'll snatch one tomorrow."

The radio in the living room squealed and the music changed. Hazel had tuned to another station. Kate Smith belted "Moonlight Bay" through the closed door, vibrating the loose panels.

"Say we get ninety," Virgil proposed. "How many ways we gonna split it?"

"Five. We'll need that many to keep everyone in line. Six, with a man at the wheel."

"Forget the man at the wheel. We'd have to have two anyway, one for each car, and we can't afford that."

"Okay, make it five. That's eighteen thousand apiece."

Virgil grinned. "Not a bad piece of change, for one day's work. How much we got in the kitty?"

"About eight thousand."

"Four grand for each of us, plus eighteen from this job. That should set us up pretty good in Mexico." Virgil put a match to yet another cigarette. "Man, them greasers is gonna get a load of some genuine rich gringos this time around. You can bet on it."

The door opened and Hazel entered, pulling the dressing gown about her. "Virgil, it's getting late. Don't you think it's time for bed?"

"Go ahead," said Virgil testily. "I'll be along later."

Alex yawned. "I'm about ready for it myself." He stretched. "How about Annie? She go to bed?"

Hazel shook her head. "No, she fell asleep on the couch. With that movie magazine on her lap. She's been reading that dumb thing over and over again since you got it for her."

"Well, as long as it gives her something to do." Alex said sleepily.

"And that's another thing. She hasn't lifted a finger to help with anything since we *got* here. Alex, she's driving me up the wall."

"I'll talk to her."

Hazel sighed shortly, dismissing the subject. "What are you two talking about?" She looked from Alex to Virgil. Virgil's eyes flickered to the map of Shawnee for an instant, then shot back to his wife. Too late. She stared at the map. "I see," she said quietly.

"Hazel, it's not what you think."

"How do you know what I think?"

Virgil leaned forward, encircling the map with his long arms. "This bank is the key to a fresh start. We can pick up and take off, leave the cops with egg on their big fat faces. Would you like that?"

"You mean Mexico, don't you? I heard you talking about it when I came in."

"That's it. Mexico. No more Public Enemy Number One. No more Tri-State Terror. Just Mr. and Mrs. Warren Henry, from Oklahoma."

"And twenty thousand dollars," added Alex.

"Why Mexico?" Hazel asked. "Why not here?"

Virgil went limp in his chair. He put his cigarette between his lips and dragged deeply on it, then let the smoke curl out his nostrils. "Have you read a newspaper lately?"

Hazel closed her eyes and nodded. "I understand."

"So we'll crack this one bank and skip. They tell me the border's a cinch. The guards are out looking for wetbacks coming in, not tourists heading out. Public Enemy Number One don't mean a thing to them. We're as good as clear right now."

They stared at each other a long time, neither of them moving or saying a word. Finally, a loud comic yawn shattered the silence and Alex got to his feet. "You two can keep sizing each other up like a snake and a mongoose, for all I care. Me for bed."

He went out and closed the door behind him, separating himself from the silent tableau within.

Twenty-six miles away, the three-car convoy hurtled and bounced along the rain-scarred road leading to Shawnee, transmissions whining dangerously. The face of the federal agent behind the wheel of the first vehicle, bathed in the eerie green glow of the dashboard lights, was tense and knotted, his eyes like slits in a Halloween mask. Farnum's cigarette glowed calmly through the darkness in the back seat.

"What about it, Chief?" someone asked. "Is this guy Ballard as tough as the papers make him out to be?"

The red glow flew to Farnum's invisible lips, brightened, then withdrew as a pall of smoke was discharged into the blackness. "He's been in business eleven years. That's tough enough, I guess."

"I guess it really doesn't matter, with fifteen men on our side." The voice was the driver's.

"That depends on how many Ballard has with him."

"The landlord says there are at least two women in that house," said the first man. The barrel of his machine gun glinted as he shifted it to his other knee. "What's the procedure with them?"

"They'll be given a chance to surrender."

"And if they don't?"

There was no answer. Farnum stirred in his seat to look out the back window. His features were thrown into brief relief as the headlights of the following car fell on his face, then faded again when he turned back. "I hope that hick sheriff knows enough to keep his boys in line," he said. "I don't trust that guy."

The convoy roared on.

Chapter Nineteen

It was 2:00 A.M. when the first car coasted to a stop three blocks from the two-story house on the edge of Shawnee. The brakes creaked. The headlights died. Behind it, the second car halted, then the third. The hissing of the rain became the only sound.

A door snicked and opened, then another and another. Guns rattled. Shoes scraped on concrete. A red glow arched through the air, came to a rest on the wet pavement, and vanished. Farnum expelled the last of his cigarette smoke. "The house is there, on the corner." He pointed, but no one could see where he was pointing. It didn't matter, because they knew he would lead them to it. "All right, let's go." They followed him in bulk.

The curtains were open on a ground floor window, a light showing through it. When they got close enough to make out the figure that was moving around within, Farnum put out a hand and stopped them.

"Jesus, it's him," someone whispered.

"Shhhh!" Farnum's warning came like a pistol shot. "Where's the sheriff?"

"Here!" Sheriff McCracken pushed his way through to the front.

"Sheriff, take your men and go around the rear. We'll take up the front. When you hear gunfire, charge in shooting."

The sheriff grunted.

The body of men split up, the uniformed deputies slogging through the drenched lawns that led toward the other side of the house on the corner. When it was silent, the federal agents move in on the lighted window.

A big spotted dog leapt up, his chain rattling, and began barking.

"That damned dog!" whispered the man at Farnum's side.

"That damned dog!" growled Virgil. He was standing near the window in his undershirt and trousers, a shoe in his hand. Hazel, who had finally managed to doze off in the bed, came awake, not because of the dog, but because of Virgil's oath. The cylindrical black oil heater in the center of the floor glowed cheerily, its yellow flame projecting a single big flower pattern through the ventilated top onto the ceiling. Virgil's converted Lugers lay peacefully on the table in front of the window.

"He'll quiet down after a while," Hazel said sleepily. "He just wants in."

"It's the neighbors I'm worried about. All we need's a call to the cops to tip over the bandwagon." He threw the shoe to the floor with a thud and bent to untie the other one.

The window burst where his head had been and something thunkered into the wall opposite. Virgil hit the floor. Hazel screamed.

"This is the law!" bellowed a voice from outside. "Put your hands up, Ballard. And don't reach for those guns!"

Virgil hesitated only a second. He sprang to his feet and grasped the two Lugers, firing them even before they had cleared the table. The window fell apart before the onslaught.

The blackness in the yard was shattered in a dozen places as yellow streaks of fire erupted from the trees and bushes.

"Down! Get under the bed!" Virgil, flattened against the wall beside the splintered window frame, shouted at Hazel. She slammed to the floor in a tangle of bedsheets and rolled beneath the big four-poster. Lead was whumping into the back wall in big handfuls, loosing a shower of plaster onto the floor with each impact.

A .45 slug blasted through the front wall and clipped Virgil in his bare right shoulder. He spun past the window and collapsed on one knee, blood streaming from the wound.

"Virgil!" screamed Hazel, struggling to get out from under the bed.

"Stay back!" he grunted and shuffled around to

the other side of the window. The wooden floor was spattered red.

"We got him!" A youthful federal agent began moving forward.

"Get back there!" spat Farnum. "He's not dead yet." The last part of his statement was lost in the din of fresh fire from the bedroom. "What'd I tell you?" said the chief, and leveled a blast with his machine gun across the shattered sill.

A second-story window on the other end of the house was wrenched upward and a machine gun began hammering from the blackened aperture. Farnum shouted and pointed in that direction. Some of the agents swung their fire to the upper part of the house, but not before Sheriff McCracken's deputies had opened up with their shotguns, slamming loads of buckshot into the whitewashed boards. Lights began to blink on in windows all up and down the residential street.

Virgil was clearing a jam in one of his Lugers when he heard the deep rattle of Alex Kern's machine gun start up on the southwest side of the house. He grinned and smacked the end of the big clip with the heel of his hand. "Good old Alex."

The room was in darkness now, Hazel having doused the bedside lamp at Virgil's command. Only the glowing design thrown across the ceiling by the oil heater remained, to cast an unreal magic-lantern effect over the whole scene of destruction.

"Virgil? Virgil, are you all right?" Hazel's voice was little more than a whisper.

The robber heaved and grunted with the effort of

readjusting the magazine. At last he panted triumphantly, and, leveling the pistol with both hands, sent a new burst into the yard. "Me and Alex, we'll take 'em."

In the bedroom on the second story, Alex was standing square in the window, describing a broad to-and-fro arc with his Thompson across the stretch of grass between their house and the one next door. His spent cartridges plinked to the floor in a steady chorus of bouncing brass. Return fire flashed in the darkness below like strings of exploding Christmas tree lights. Only six more shopping days till Christmas, he thought wryly as he sent a sustained burst in the direction of the street.

Annabelle, squeezed close to the wall in her bedcovers, screamed loud and long, stopping at intervals only long enough to take a breath. Her movie magazine lay in tatters on the floor, where it had landed after having been shot off the night table by a lawman's errant bullet. Her husband, enveloped in darkness and clinging gunsmoke, looked more to her like a demon released from the hell her family deacon used to preach about than the personable young rake she had married. She felt she was on the wrong side.

"Damn place is like a fortress." Farnum dropped his submachine gun to knee-level in order to bring the circulation back into his arms, then raised it again and blasted at Ballard's bedroom window. Beneath and through the din of battle, the big pointer remained standing at the end of his chain, barking and yelping at the team of invaders. The special agent cursed him between bursts.

"Where are those men with the gas?" He screamed the question into the ear of the man nearest him.

" 'Round the corner, with the rest of the hicks," was the reply.

"Get 'em."

The subordinate scrambled to his feet and went running off in that direction, crouching beneath the crossfire.

Except for the two who had joined the sheriff's deputies for the assault on the second story, and the one Farnum had sent off to get the tear gas, all the federal men were firing into the bedroom of the Tri-State Terror. *What the hell's holding him up?* thought Farnum as he blasted away, feeling the heat of the machine gun's barrel through the wooden forward grip.

The agent returned with one of the deputies, who held a short, wire-barreled shotgunlike weapon cradled in his big hands. They huddled around the chief.

Farnum pointed at the bullet-smashed window. "Lob a canister through there and run like hell."

The man grunted, leveled the wire barrel at the window, and squeezed the trigger. Pom! Something big erupted from the muzzle and went sailing over the sill into the shadowy chamber. The two agents and the deputy straightened and leaped backward just as fresh fire opened up from one of the converted Lugers. When they stopped running at the edge of the yard, volumes of yellowish smoke came billowing out through the window, curling and expanding as it overflowed the dimensions of the bedroom. Someone was coughing at the center of the cloud.

Farnum stood back facing the front door just yards from the infernal smoke and motioned his men to spread out. "Get ready," he snapped.

Alex heard the strange whumping noise from around the corner and wondered what it was. He could still detect the rapid brrrp of Virgil's pistols, so he decided that everything was all right in that direction. As for himself, he was doing all right, since most of the men below were armed only with shotguns, and by the time their fire reached his level, the pellets had spread out so that they weren't too much of a threat.

He had caught a tiny bit of lead in his right forearm, but it was little more than a bee sting to him as he concentrated upon keeping the deputies back beyond effective shotgun range. Now and then a federal man got in a good burst with a Thompson, which was lethal enough at any range, but, since it was almost impossible to aim a machine gun beyond the space of a few yards, Alex felt pretty safe. The window, which he had shoved upward to begin the battle, hadn't even been broken. Now if only Annabelle would stop screaming, he could maybe lay down a good enough pattern of fire to back off the lawmen long enough for him to escape.

He whirled and snapped his wife a furious glance through the enveloping darkness. "Shut up, damn it! How do you expect me to concentrate if—" He was just turning back to rejoin the battle when a bucketload of .45-caliber lead slammed into his chest. He screamed, staggered backward, wavered on unsteady legs, and pitched forward out through the window. His body did a single somersault in the air and splatted facedown on the wet grass. His machine gun came down afterward, bouncing twice against the wall before it landed clattering in the paved driveway. Annabelle stopped screaming as if someone had flipped a switch.

The gray steel tear-gas canister zinged through the window as Virgil was reloading one of his pistols. It hit the floor and bounded end over end, leading a spiral of yellow smoke from a fissure in its top. The room was hazy with the gas by the time Virgil dived after the offending object, seeking to sling it back outside. He scrabbled around on his hands and knees, groping for it, his eyes stinging, his throat threatening to turn itself inside out. The wound in his arm throbbed painfully as new blood washed over the sticky fluid that had dried over his right side. He began coughing horribly and staggered to his feet, grasping his reloaded gun from the smoke-enshrouded floor. "We got to clear out!" he choked, groping for the door.

The space between the bed and the floor was airless, an almost tangible slab of smoke crammed into it. Hazel had crawled out and was blindly attempting to stand up. It wasn't easy. Her face and eyes burned and the moist parts of her body were aflame, the panic born of pain making her slip and slide, driving splinters deep into her bare hands and feet from the plank floor. She heard the doorknob rattle, felt the rush of fresh air invade the room, and dragged herself laboriously to her feet, calling unintelligibly into the thickening fog. "Virgil! Where are you? Are you here? Virgil?" She clawed the empty air.

The fresh air in the hallway was delicious. Virgil stood there a moment, drawing in lungfuls of it, then ran for the kitchen, his stockinged feet padding on the worn linoleum. He was thinking about the black Pontiac parked in the garage, loaded with machine guns and shotguns, tank full of gas. Hazel would be all right; the law never touched women. He'd come back later and get her. Then Mexico. Maybe Alex would be along too, if he escaped tonight.

When he got to the kitchen and the back door, he found it shot apart, hanging precariously on its smashed hinges, more bullets coming through even as he took note of it. The lawmen were here too. Their machine guns rattled away as if they knew what they were shooting at. Every few seconds, the full-throated roar of a shotgun would sound, its impact splintering what remained of the sideboards and rattling the crockery in the kitchen. Virgil about-faced and headed back down the hallway in the direction of the front door. Tear gas was seeping in from the bedroom in greater volumes than before, meaning that another canister had been fired. He hurried past.

Hazel ran through the smoke-enshrouded doorway and collided with Virgil. Her eyes were red and swollen and her black hair was plastered damply against her head. Her transparent negligee clung immodestly to her body. "Virgil!" she cried. "Don't go out there! They'll kill you!" She clung desperately to him.

He struggled with her. The gaping wound in his shoulder had sapped his strength. "Out of my way! I'll be back for you!"

She held on. "We've got the money! We can get lawyers! Virgil, there's no need to run!"

"Get away!" Virgil shoved her away with a mighty effort. She staggered backward and fell down. He leaped over her and bolted for the front door. He paused with his hand on the knob and looked back at her. "Lawyers ain't for guys like me," he said, and held up the big Luger. "*This* is my way." He studied her a moment longer, then swung open the door and dived out.

Hazel looked up and saw Annabelle standing at the top of the staircase. She looked like a ghost, her eyes large and dull, her soaked flannel nightgown held about her neck in one gaunt hand. "Alex's gone," she said simply, as new gunfire exploded from the front.

The machine guns of the federal agents were trained on the low veranda when the door opened. There was a pause, during which Farnum caught his breath and held it, his fine nostrils quivering spasmodically. The rain sizzled loudly on the grass and shrubs. Then a gray figure fluttered into sight and leaped over the wooden porch railing. "Fire!" Farnum led the fussilade by a microsecond. The wooden steps flew apart in a flurry of mud and splinters. The dim figure staggered and fell forward onto his hands and knees. *We got him,* he thought. *We got him, we got him, we got him.*

Virgil coughed and shook his head. The grass felt damp, and some of it was his blood. His rib cage was smashed, the splintered bones drawing in and out with each breath. He sucked in a chestful of air, grasped his gun more tightly, and threw himself up off the ground. *You bastards, you dirty bastards, I'm gonna survive.* He ripped off two short bursts and ran.

"He's headed out—on a getaway!" One of the younger agents jerked off a desperate blast at the fleeing figure. It missed a step, weaved for a few paces, and picked up momentum.

He was past the garage now, and was rapidly closing the gap between himself and the maze of suburban dwellings. Streaks of fire flashed through the curtain of night, picking at the ground around the fugitive, slamming into the trunks of trees, whanging through the garage's solid doors, ricocheting off the street and sidewalk. The explosions echoed up and down the residential block like a symphony of oversize kettle drums.

"Get the sonuvabitch!" screamed Farnum. *What the hell is holding him up?* He squinted through the rain, trying to keep his eyes on the ghostly figure racing toward the back of the house next door. Once he thought he saw him slump forward again, then get up and run on. In the next instant he was gone, hidden by the corner of the neighboring dwelling.

"We got him!" shouted a trenched-coated agent standing in the middle of the street. He was the one who had uttered the same words not twenty minutes before.

"Did you see him fall?" Farnum retorted.

"Yes, sir. Right there. By that house."

"Get the hell down there and take a look." He felt

a hand on his arm and started around. It was Sheriff McCracken.

"We got Kern," he told the agent curtly. "Think there's any more in there?"

Farnum was watching the movements of the agent's flashlight near the corner of the next house. "Get some more gas in there and we'll see. Use it up."

"All of it?"

"Fill it to the top." He brought his collar up around his ears.

The sheriff nodded and moved off.

The agent with the flashlight returned, shaking his head. "Nothing, sir. He's gone." He had to shout to be heard over the bam of the tear-gas rifles.

Smoke began to billow from the smashed windows. Farnum watched it intently. "All right. We'll look for him." The young agent sniffed his approval and left to assist the other lawmen.

Two women came out onto the porch, coughing and holding their hands aloft. The men gathered around them cautiously, guns raised.

Farnum ran his eyes over the scene, now thrown into faint illumination by the overlapping circles of light from porch lights on both sides of the street. He took in the smashed walls and ragged windows, studied the damaged trees and the bullet-chewed front lawn, finally spotted the broken body in the puddle of blood and water, and went up to talk with the captured women. The weather was lousy.

The side door of the shop gave way with a feeble kick. Virgil stumbled over the threshold and found himself in complete darkness, the night closing in on him like the walls of a vise. Water streamed from his clothes and spattered on the plank floor. Or was it blood? Blood from his two busted legs. That bastard Nelson Garver.

He made his way through the building, feet dragging, the humming in his ears becoming unbearable. He gripped the pistol tighter in his hands. *You're in a lot of trouble, son.* The voice was soft, almost paternal. *An armed robbery charge like this will get you sent up, you know that?* That damned bartender. One hundred and fifty jugs of Oklahoma White Lightning bought at a bargain, and then he goes and files a charge against him for armed robbery. He bumped into something hard and cursed.

The back part of the shop was open, free of obstacles and dangerous projections. Virgil staggered to the center. He felt something soft against his knees, reached down and felt it with his hands. Then he grunted and threw himself headlong across the bed.

That sonuvabitch with a face like a ferret. *We're gonna find you a place to stay. Ain't that nice?* Virgil tried to spit in the narrow, sneering face that floated before him, but his mouth was dry. The best he could do was hiss.

Hit the small towns, the one-street burgs. Who could have expected Roscoe Hunter to run out like that? Roy was right. You never know when they're gonna be tearing up the streets in those big cities. They killed Boyd in Kansas City. I told him not to wear that damn vest.

It was getting darker. How can it get darker when it's pitch-black already? Worth thinking about. Damn sheet's getting wet. Roof must leak. Sticky, too. That bastard Nelson Garver. The bed began to move, and Virgil knew he was lying between the front and back seats of a Saxon six. *Missouri comin' up.*

The pistol felt heavy in his hand. *Some gun, huh?* Thompson submachine gun, .45 caliber, 1600 rounds per minute. Really make the cops run with this one. It fell to the floor with a thump. Get it later.

It's not just the banks. Hazel looked at him, her face a mixture of anger and anguish. *You've escaped from three prisons. You're wanted for the murders of three men ... Virgil, isn't that enough?* No, Hazel, not nearly enough.

It came while he was reliving the Dawes bank job, between watching Floyd Moss guarding the outside with his sawed-off shotgun and noticing that old constable, Ed Fellows, coming over from Fred Benson's service station. He felt cold for a second, unbearably cold—and then, suddenly, he was warm. This, he thought, must be the moment. But he never finished the thought. It sure was warm.

The sheriff kneels, dips his fingers in the blood. It is fresh. Straightening, he taps two of his deputies on their shoulders and jerks his head to indicate the darkened furniture shop that looms quietly over the narrow street, its big plate window made opaque by a drawn shade. The deputies nod their understanding and signal to the others. In the charcoal-gray of early morning, the search for Virgil Ballard comes to a halt.

"We know you're in there, Ballard." The sheriff's voice is awkward through hours of unuse. He clears his throat raspingly before going on. "Throw out

your gun and come out with your hands in the air."
The rain patters through the stretch of silence. After
two minutes, the lawman indicates the first two
deputies. "Go around back and force your way in."

When they have gone, McCracken sweeps his
eyes around the rest of the men and grasps his shotgun tightly. The others understand. They reach the
glass-paneled door and wait. Water seeps through
between the rolled awning and the wall of the shop
and bleeds down the black window like nervous
perspiration.

There is a crash from inside the shop. The deputy
nearest the door responds by kicking and bursting
the lock, and the lawmen rush inside. They pause in
the opening, shotguns ready. The interior is a jumble of indistinct black shapes with a wide aisle cutting through them to the back of the shop. The light
is gray and indistinct, filtering in through the
smashed door and lying across the scene like a dam-
pened sheet.

"Back here, Sheriff." The voice comes from the
back of the shop. "We found him."

Lanky Jake is the first to reach the open space
before the back door. He whistles. The sheriff is
next, followed by the rest of the deputies.

The two men who had come in the back stand on
the other side of the bed display, looking like pall-
bearers at a funeral. Virgil Ballard is stretched facedown across the bed. His face is buried in the pillow,
partially obscured by his disheveled blond hair.
The converted Luger lies on the floor, inches beneath
the fingers of his limp hand. The blood on the
tangled bedsheets is still fresh.

"He must of taken a pound of lead." Jake's voice is hushed.

"Blood till hell won't have it," drawls another.

The sheriff nudges the thick-set deputy at his side. "Go get the feds." The deputy withdraws grudgingly.

"Lookit his legs." An older deputy directs his flashlight on the foot of the bed. The pin-striped trouser legs are stained an ugly brown.

Jake hisses an astonished oath. "Christ, how'd he get this far on two busted legs?"

The sheriff places a fat cigar between his teeth and lights it. "Them kind of people ain't human. That's how they keep goin'." He shrugs it off and turns away, blowing volumes of gray smoke toward the open front door. "Jeez, will you lookit that rain? Probably keep it up all day long."